# Jessamy looked at Luke with hostility

"I'm afraid I'm not very well versed in the kind of games you play," she protested.

"Games?" he said softly.

"Well, what else would you call it when you invite your girl friend along and then try to make love to me?" she choked.

"Jealous, Jessamy?" There was a light in his eyes that made her heart beat faster, but she was determined that this time she wasn't going to let him get through her defenses.

"Jealous? Don't flatter yourself," she flung at him.

He moved swiftly, taking her so completely by surprise she had no chance to guard against the leaping response to his deep, searching kiss. He raised his head, and there was the light of victory in his eyes. "Oh, but I think you are."

# WELCOME
# TO THE WONDERFUL WORLD
## OF *Harlequin Romances*

Interesting, informative and entertaining, each Harlequin Romance portrays an appealing and original love story. With a varied array of settings, we may lure you on an African safari, to a quaint Welsh village, or an exotic Riviera location—anywhere and everywhere that adventurous men and women fall in love.

As publishers of Harlequin Romances, we're extremely proud of our books. Since 1949, Harlequin Enterprises has built its publishing reputation on the solid base of quality and originality. Our stories are the most popular paperback romances sold in North America; every month, six new titles are released and sold at nearly every book-selling store in Canada and the United States.

A free catalogue listing all Harlequin Romances can be yours by writing to the

HARLEQUIN READER SERVICE,
(In the U.S.) 2504 West Southern Avenue, Tempe, AZ 85282
(In Canada) Stratford, Ontario, N5A 6W2

We sincerely hope you enjoy reading this Harlequin Romance.

Yours truly,

THE PUBLISHERS
*Harlequin Romances*

# Knave
# of Hearts

## Stacy Absalom

# Harlequin Books

TORONTO • NEW YORK • LONDON
AMSTERDAM • PARIS • SYDNEY • HAMBURG
STOCKHOLM • ATHENS • TOKYO • MILAN

Original hardcover edition published in 1983
by Mills & Boon Limited

ISBN 0-373-02581-5

Harlequin Romance first edition November 1983

Printed in U.S.A.

# CHAPTER ONE

AFTERWARDS she felt there should have been some premonition, a sixth sense warning her that after today nothing would ever be quite the same again. But on that warm, sunny morning in early May, Jessamy Daunay felt nothing but the usual lift of her spirits as she stepped out on to the deck.

The sun picked out the bright red and green paintwork of her converted narrow-boat home, moored on the sleepy, tree-fringed lagoon running off the canal. Across the lagoon the ground rose steeply to a horizon dominated by the picturesque ruin of what had once been the lock-keeper's cottage that marked the top of the flight of locks carrying the main canal down the hill to the junction with the local arm that ran only as far as Market Swinford at the bottom. The bright sunlight even lent a glamour to the huddle of buildings where the two canals met, the small inn, the gift and souvenir shop, the booking office and the long, low repair sheds of the marina.

Jessamy had to admit that her first sight of the rather shabby little marina had been daunting, but working for Barry Hanson for the last ten months she had become infected by his enthusiasm and vision. Now she saw it all with his eyes, imagining it as it would be one day when he could find the capital to improve it.

Often during the winter months when business was slack she had listened enthralled while Barry dreamed aloud of how he would like to move the repair sheds out of sight behind the belt of trees, how he meant to refurbish the old inn, modernising it but leaving in all the old-world features like the oak beams, the small-paned windows and the inglenook fireplaces, how he planned to build a fine new restaurant on at the back and put Jessamy in charge so at last she would have real scope for her culinary talents, how perhaps later he might even build some holiday chalets among the trees and turn the place into a real leisure centre.

His oil-ingrained mechanic's hands had drawn rough plans which he explained to her with an enthusiasm that lit his rather homely features and left his mop of sun and wind-bleached curls even more unruly, his usual taciturn nature waxing lyrical over the fortune that was waiting to be made.

And if anyone deserved to make a fortune it was Barry Hanson, Jessamy thought with fierce loyalty as she wheeled her bicycle down the gangplank from her houseboat to the towpath running alongside. Out of all the prospective employers who had interviewed her during her long months of unemployment after she graduated from her catering and Cordon Bleu cookery course, Barry had been the only one to actually offer her a job.

The bar snacks and inexpensive meals that were all she was called upon to provide for the visitors to this out-of-the-way beauty spot didn't even begin to use all her skills, and the pay was small, but she would always be grateful to Barry for giving her this chance. She was very well aware that even the small wage he paid her stretched his resources, and she was prepared to work all hours to justify his faith in her.

Already many of the local people who used the walk beside the flight of locks and dropped into the little waterside inn for a cup of coffee or a beer were being tempted by her delicious quiches, her crusty home-made bread, her mouthwatering pizzas and imaginative salads. But there just weren't enough of them. And although the awakening interest in the inland waterways over the last few years had increased the trade in hiring out cruisers for the day or running weekend and evening narrow-boat trips during the summer, the marina still wasn't making enough money for Barry to plough back into improving the place and so attract more customers.

It was a vicious circle, Jessamy thought as she got on her bicycle and began to pedal along the rutted track that was the only road from the marina to the village. Without more customers they couldn't hope to make enough money to improve the place, and without improvements they were unlikely to attract more customers. She only hoped Barry wouldn't lose faith in his dream. She couldn't help noticing that for the last few weeks he'd worn a worried frown, and he hadn't once mentioned any of his plans.

But it was too beautiful a morning for such pessimistic thoughts. Milk-chocolate-coloured cows raised their heads from the lush grass to watch her curiously as she cycled past, and a lark poured out his exuberant song at the blue arch of the sky. The chestnut trees around the old grey stone church were just coming into flower. In another week they would be laden with their pink 'candles'.

As she turned out of the track on to the village street she was greeted by everyone she passed; the butcher, pulling out his awning to shade his window against the sun that promised to be hot later and the postman who'd stopped to gossip with him; Mrs Lush, cleaning the windows of her little sub-post office with brawny arms; old Mr Carron weeding his tiny cottage garden and several children on their way to school. It gave her a warm feeling of belonging, as if the whole community were her family, a feeling Jessamy appreciated as all the real family she had now were on the other side of the world ever since her widowed mother had gone out to Australia to live with Jessamy's brother and his wife.

It was as she reached the turning down to the market

garden that the accident happened. There was usually little traffic on that road, but afterwards Jessamy had to admit she was careless. She had just begun to make her right turn when suddenly she realised there was a car hurtling towards her round the bend. And such a car! It was a gleaming cream and chromium pre-war Jáguar, its enormous headlamps and snarling radiator grill giving it the look of a predatory beast.

If she had kept going she would have made it across, but she was so startled she hesitated and wobbled. As the car screeched to a halt the chromium-plated bumper just nudged her rear wheel, sending her sprawling on the grass verge.

She lay there winded as a car door slammed and what appeared to be a dark, thunderous-faced giant loomed over her.

'What the hell do you think you're playing at?' he yelled furiously. 'Wobbling along the middle of the road as if you owned it!'

'Me?' Jessamy gasped indignantly. 'That's a lethal weapon you're driving, especially on country roads like this. You were travelling much too fast, you roadhog!'

'If I *had* been travelling too fast, you wouldn't be here to tell the tale,' he retorted coldly. 'I'm surprised at your mother letting you out on a bike when you obviously have no road sense!'

Jessamy glared back at him, quite unaware that with her slight figure clad in bright pink dungarees sprawling in a most undignified position, her natural blonde hair tied up in a ponytail and her face innocent of make-up, she looked nearer to fifteen than her twenty-three years.

'And you obviously never had a mother!' she spat at him, knowing she was being unforgivably rude but too angry to care. Why did he have to stand over her like some avenging god? And he hadn't even asked her if she was hurt! Probably far more concerned about whether his precious car was scratched, she thought, aggrieved. And indeed it would be a pity if the car was damaged. It must be forty-five years old if it was a day, and in absolutely immaculate condition.

'Are you hurt?' he asked, looking slightly less angry.

'No thanks to you if I'm not,' Jessamy muttered, scrambling to her feet and shrugging off his hand when he would have helped.

'Just a bit grass-stained, and that'll wash out,' he said briskly, brushing grass and dead leaves from her knees as if she really was the child he obviously thought her. 'You've been lucky this time, but don't take such risks again.'

She longed to make a dent in his patronising arrogance, but could find nothing scathing enough to say. Standing as she did at her full height of five feet two and a quarter inches plus the heels of her pink sandals, the top of her head didn't quite reach his shoulder. And it wasn't just his height that made her feel so inadequate. From the top of his head where the dark hair sprang from a widow's peak in a casual cut that fell just short of his collar to the handmade shoes on his feet, he exuded wealth and authority, though she judged him to be no more than thirty-two or three.

Anyone who drove a car like the Jaguar would have to be rich beyond her wildest dreams, and his clothes bore that opinion out. The dark grey business suit that fitted his broad shoulders so snugly could only have come from a top London tailor, and his shirt and matching tie looked like pure silk. And as for the gold cufflinks peeping from his cuff, she thought sourly, if he fell in the canal he'd sink straight to the bottom under the weight.

'Your bike seems to be all right too,' he said, apparently unaware of her scrutiny. He wheeled it a little way along the lane. 'Though I think you ought to get your father to check the brakes,' he added as he wheeled it back again.

'There's nothing wrong with the brakes,' she snapped, snatching the bike from him and preparing to ride away. 'So don't try to put the blame for your careless driving on that!' As she pushed off along the lane she heard his footsteps retreating. The car door slammed and he roared off.

Now that his disturbing presence had departed she had to admit that the near-accident had been as much her fault as his. But even so, she thought resentfully, that didn't give him the right to act like a lord of creation and treat her like a ragamuffin child.

She was still seething when she reached the market garden and found an even bigger shock waiting for her there.

The market garden was run by Joe Sutherland and his two sons, and Jessamy bought most of her salad stuffs and fresh vegetables there. Usually she was assured of a cheerful welcome and prompt attention when she went in with her order, but this time the youngest son, Mike, on his own in the packing shed, turned bright pink when he saw her.

'I'd better go and get Dad,' he said.

'But it's only my usual order, Mike.' He'd often served her before. 'Unless your courgettes are ready yet . . .'

He shuffled his feet in embarrassment and turned an even brighter pink as he repeated, 'I'd better go and get him,' before scuttling out of the packing shed like a startled rabbit.

'What on earth's the matter with Mike this morning, Joe?' Jessamy asked in some amusement as the big man stumped into the shed in his wellington boots a few moments later.

'He was only obeying instructions, Miss.' Joe Sutherland looked almost as embarrassed as his son. 'The fact is, we can't let you go on having stuff like this.'

She stared at him uncomprehendingly. 'You mean you're not selling your produce any more?'

'Oh, we're *selling* it all right. You can *buy* as much as you like,' he blustered. 'But damn it all, we can't go on giving the stuff away!'

Jessamy felt as if an icy stone had been dropped into her stomach. 'Oh, Joe! You mean your bill hasn't been paid?'

'Not for the last three months,' Joe said grimly. 'Look, I know it's not your fault, m'dear, and I hate having to say this to you, but our costs are rising all the time. We just can't afford to go on subsidising that marina, you must see that.'

'Yes, Joe. Yes, of course I see that . . .' She felt sick, remembering that worried frown Barry had been wearing for several weeks now.

She knew of course that the marina was run on a shoestring, but she'd had no idea things were so bad that Barry was having difficulty paying his bills. Surely if the marina was running into real trouble he would have told her?

And what could be bigger trouble than having no food to offer their customers? It was Saturday tomorrow and the weekends were always their busiest time, especially when the weather was good.

'Look, Joe . . .' she pleaded desperately, digging into her purse to make sure she had enough money with her, 'I'm sure it's an oversight—Barry's had a lot on his mind lately. How about if I pay cash for today's order? I promise I'll chase him up right away about settling the outstanding account.'

'Well . . . I suppose it'll be all right,' Joe conceded.

Thoughts scurried round Jessamy's head like frantic mice as she pedalled back through the village. Why hadn't Barry told her if he was getting into financial difficulties? Didn't he know she would be prepared to work for just her bed and board if that would help to keep things going?

But if there was no money to pay the suppliers' bills, what use was a cook to him? She felt sick at heart at the thought that she might have to leave this lovely place and all the friends she'd made here. And what about Barry? He'd put everything he had, including his heart and soul, into making a success of the marina. Please God she was wrong and Joe Sutherland's unpaid account was just an oversight.

Jessamy had almost reached the turning that led off to the marina when a gleam of cream and chrome caught her eye. She braked to a halt. It was the pre-war Jaguar car and it was parked on the grass verge among the bushes, almost as if an attempt had been made to hide it! Looking around for the owner, she was puzzled when there seemed to be no sign of him.

She shrugged. The motives of a man so obviously accustomed to having his own way were beyond her simple mind, and anyway, she had far more pressing things to worry about.

Not waiting to take her bicycle back to the boat or even to unpack the salad stuffs from the carrier at the back, she leaned it against the wall of the inn and hurried in to tell Barry what had happened at the market garden.

But as she burst into the small, cluttered office, the man she surprised bending over the filing cabinet going systematically through the marina's private papers wasn't Barry. It was the driver of the Jaguar car, Mr Gold Cufflinks himself!

Jessamy stopped dead in outrage. 'What the blazes do you think you're doing?'

He turned unhurriedly to face her, but though his dark eyebrows rose at her challenge, he didn't look in the least bit guilty at being caught in the act.

'You again! I hope you're not going to make a habit of popping up out of nowhere. Who are you anyway?'

His eyes flicked over her coolly, for all the world as if it was she who was the intruder.

So cool was he, and with such an air of authority, that for just a moment she hesitated uncertainly, until she remembered that distinctive car tucked away at the side of the road well out of sight of anyone at the marina. If he'd gone to that trouble he couldn't be up to any good.

'Never mind who I am. More to the point, who are you?' she spluttered, staggered at his nerve. 'And what are you doing snooping round a private office?'

'Snooping?' The eyes narrowed and the muscles of his chin hardened. With one hand he slid the heavy metal drawer of the filing cabinet shut and moved towards her, and for the first time Jessamy realised her vulnerability, confronting an intruder alone like this. He didn't look like a burglar, but then as far as she knew she'd never met one before. But she was apprehensively aware of the muscular shoulders beneath the well cut suit and immaculate shirt, the sheer strength and forceful power of the man.

She took a step back, her heart hammering against her ribs, but rather than let him see her fear she said with a touch of bravado, 'If it's money you're after, you're out of luck. There isn't too much of that around here.'

'I had worked that out for myself.' The stranger actually looked amused, then to disconcert her still further he added, 'Perhaps Mr Hanson will explain that I'm not a sneak-thief after the takings.'

Jessamy turned quickly as Barry came into the office, a Barry she hardly recognised, wearing a suit and tie instead of his usual oil-stained jeans and tee-shirt and with his unruly mop of fair hair slicked down into a semblance of tidiness. His face was red with embarrassment and he shot an apologetic glance at the stranger as he said, 'Jess, what on earth have you been saying? Surely you didn't really accuse——'

'Well, what else was I to think?' she broke in defensively. 'I found this man alone here rifling the filing cabinet, going through your private papers.'

'So she tackled me without a second thought,' the stranger said with amusement still lingering in his eyes. 'I swear if you hadn't come in just then she'd have had me helpless in a half-nelson!'

He was mocking her. She had been the helpless one and he knew it. If he *had* been up to no good she wouldn't have stood a chance against him. He could have overpowered her in seconds. She shivered. She wasn't after all in danger of being hit over the head, yet her heart was still beating uncomfortably fast. There was something about this man, something she found deeply disturbing, even threatening.

'I'm sorry about the misunderstanding.' Barry was apologising for her. 'This is Jessamy Daunay, the girl I was telling you about. She's cook, barmaid and general assistant around here. A real jewel. Jess, this is Luke Monro. He——' He paused as if the words were sticking in his throat. 'Mr Monro is the new owner of the marina.'

Jessamy stared at him thunderstruck. 'The new owner?' she echoed in disbelief. 'But——' That he was in some difficulty she couldn't help but be aware, especially after this morning's humiliating incident at the market garden over the unpaid bill, but never once had he mentioned the possibility of giving up. 'Barry, you *can't* be thinking of selling! Not to him!' Her eyes seemed to be drawn to the tall figure who dominated the small office.

'Not thinking of it,' Luke Monro said. 'The deal was completed yesterday. So you see, Miss Daunay, I had every right to be "snooping" in the filing cabinet.'

Her cheeks burned under his mocking gaze. 'Yesterday?' She turned a look of agonised reproach at Barry. 'You never said a word! You might have warned me, Barry.'

'For once I agree with Miss Daunay. I was certainly under the impression that all the staff had been informed of developments by now, Hanson. Or were you hoping this little problem too would go away?' There was a sardonic curl to his mouth as Luke Monro tossed the sheaf of papers he was holding on to the littered desk. 'I'll give you five minutes to explain to Miss Daunay exactly how things stand.'

'Bastard!' Barry muttered as the door closed with a snap. Up to that moment his manner towards Luke Monro had been conciliating, and Jessamy was shocked at the sudden bitter expletive.

'If you don't like him then why on earth did you sell to him? Why the sudden decision to sell anyway, when you had such marvellous plans for this place?'

'Because I didn't have any option,' he said wearily. His sudden burst of rancour seemed to have burned itself out and in its place was a kind of defeated bewilderment. 'He ran rings round me, Jess. I didn't even know he was still interested in the marina.'

'*Still* interested?'

'He tried to get me to sell a couple of years ago, but of course I turned him down. I'd no idea he'd gone behind my back and bought the property without me knowing.'

'Hang on a minute,' she said sharply. 'How could he have bought your property without you knowing it?'

'Not *my* property . . . the landlord's. I only lease the land and buildings, you know. If I *had* owned it all I'd be laughing. I'd have no trouble in raising the capital to make all the improvements I wanted. And Monro wouldn't have been able to put me out of business.'

'But surely,' Jessamy frowned, 'even if the ownership of the property has changed hands, you still have rights as a tenant.'

'I was on a three year lease,' Barry said dully, 'which was due for renewal on the first of this month. Monro refused to renew it, so all I was left with was a few boats and a whopping great overdraft at the bank.'

'But that's sharp practice!' Jessamy was appalled that anyone could be so underhand and unscrupulous.

'He calls it good business. And I have to admit the price he paid for the boats and the goodwill of the business was very fair,' Barry conceded.

'Fair!' Jessamy almost choked. She could see by the bleakness on Barry's face how it was breaking his heart to lose the business he had striven so hard to make a success of, and she hated Luke Monro for doing this to him. Mr Moneybags. He only had to write out a cheque and anything he wanted was his, including someone's dream. What did he know or care of the sweat and toil that had gone into it, or the dreams he was shattering? Her instinctive dislike of the man had been proved right. Luke Monro was not a man to be trusted.

'Barry, I am sorry.' She laid a sympathetic hand on his arm. 'I wish you'd told me what was going on, though. Together we might have been able to think of something to put a spoke in his wheel.' She couldn't imagine what, as her resources were even smaller than Barry's, but at least she could have offered him moral support. 'I'd noticed you weren't your usual breezy self these last few weeks, but I never suspected anything was radically wrong till Joe Sutherland refused me any more credit this morning.'

'Joe Sutherland did that!' Barry looked shocked and not a little guilty. 'What happened?'

She explained, playing it down. Not for anything would she let on how humiliated she had felt. Barry had enough on his plate without upsetting him on her account.

But he was still stricken with remorse. 'I'm sorry, Jess. I *should* have let you know what was going on. Pride, I suppose. After the lines I'd been shooting on what I meant to do with the place I couldn't bring myself to admit I was a failure.'

'You're not a failure,' she protested with fierce loyalty. And even if it could be described as failure, it was more admirable than Luke Monro's kind of success.

'Thanks for the vote of confidence.' He grinned weakly, then the tired, defeated expression settled on his face again. 'I reckon Monro hit the nail on the head when he asked if I'd hoped the problem would just go away. Maybe there was *something* I might have done if I'd shifted myself.'

Jessamy had never seen Barry depressed before. His was an optimistic nature, over-optimistic at times, and she did have to admit he had a tendency to solve problems by pretending they didn't exist.

To try to shake him out of his mood she said. 'What are you going to do now? Will there be enough money for you to start again somewhere else?'

He gave a hollow laugh. 'Not a hope! No, by the time I've paid off the bank and settled my outstanding debts . . . by the way, don't forget to let me have the bill for the stuff you paid for this morning. It'll take a day or two, but I'll pay it off with the rest.'

'You don't have to worry about that,' Jessamy said at once. 'If you hadn't given me a job here I'd probably still be on the dole. I'm only too glad to be able to help you out in return.'

'Don't talk daft, girl.' Barry squeezed her shoulders affectionately. 'I'm not on the breadline yet. As I said, there'll be enough money to clear all my debts with a bit to spare. *And* I still have a job. Monro's asked me to stay on.'

'And you're going to?' She stared at him incredulously. 'You're prepared to stay on as hired help in the business you once owned? You're willing to work for a man like Luke Monro, after what he did to you?'

'You don't sound very pleased with the idea, Miss Daunay,' the voice that was becoming only too hatefully familiar said behind her. 'Perhaps you'd rather he joined the ranks of the unemployed?'

Jessamy whirled round and was just about to say something scathing about people who walked in on private conversations without knocking when she remembered this was his office now. Her spontaneous antipathy towards Luke Monro had been reinforced by what she had just learned of his ruthlessness and greed, and the idea of Barry being exploited by such a man made her sick with fury.

'Jess, I need this job.' Barry looked alarmed as if he anticipated her outburst and hunched his shoulders defensively. 'Maybe I wasn't cut out to be a businessman.'

'You can say that again!' Luke Monro picked up the folder he had tossed on the desk before he'd left them to their brief discussion. 'Do you realise that more than half the evening boat trips last summer ran at a loss when you take into account the suppers provided?'

'The weather let us down last summer.' Jessamy leapt to Barry's defence. 'And the suppers were my idea. I thought people might still turn out even on a cold, damp evening, if there was good food provided.'

He ignored her as if she was of less account than the fly buzzing against the windowpane. 'And most of the boat repairs you undertook during the winter,' he accused Barry. 'You didn't charge anywhere near an economic price for your labour. And as for your accounts system ... any business that allows its customers three months' credit before it even sends out a bill deserves to fail.'

Barry's rugged face reddened and his hands clenched, but all he said was, 'Well, maybe I didn't pay as much attention as I should to the books. But there were always so many other things to do.'

Jessamy seethed. Was this what it was going to be

like from now on? Barry meekly taking everything his new lord and master arrogantly handed out?

'It's all very well for you to criticise, but you know nothing at all about running a marina!' She was unable to contain herself any longer. 'You come marching in here with your big-business ideas and your moneybags as if you know it all! Well, let me tell you . . . if Barry hadn't undercut the prices the boatyard at Market Swinford would have charged, he wouldn't have got the work. So you're in for a rude awakening if you think——' She broke off abruptly when Barry kicked her sharply on the ankle and hissed, 'Shut up, you idiot!'

'I'm afraid all this has come as a bit of a shock to Jess,' he said placatingly to the bristling man behind the desk. 'So you must forgive her if she lets her loyalty run away with her. She's always been a very hardworking and devoted employee, and I'm sure she'll be just as loyal to you if you take her on.'

Jessamy gaped at him. She'd been so shattered by the news that Barry had sold the marina, so incensed at the unjust way he'd been forced into it, so spitting mad at Luke Monro's overbearing arrogance, she hadn't given a thought to her own position.

A cold hand gripped her heart. She was going to be out of a job! Nothing was more certain than that, for from the first moment she'd set eyes on Luke Monro she'd been telling him exactly what she thought of him.

She stole an apprehensive glance at him, only to find those hard eyes studying her as if she was a specimen under a microscope. She squirmed, her cheeks flaming, and longed to be able to tell him what he could do with his job. Only the full realisation of the consequences made her keep her tongue between her teeth. The houseboat she lived on went with the job. If she lost the job, not only would she have to leave this lovely place where she had begun to put down roots but she would also be without a roof over her head.

She suffered his scrutiny in seething silence, but when he said carelessly, 'I'm sure she'll do well enough as a barmaid or waitress, but you can't seriously expect me to put a girl straight from school in charge of my new restaurant kitchen,' her hackles rose again.

Before she could help herself she burst out, 'You've suggested I'm not old enough to be let out of leading reins once before this morning. I'll have you know I'm twenty-three years old and not only do I hold an advanced catering diploma but I came out top student of a Cordon Bleu cookery course!'

'Such a ripe old age!' His eyebrows arched in amusement and though he didn't actually laugh at her she could see a muscle twitching beside his mouth. 'Your qualifications are impressive, Miss Daunay, but I still think the kind of food I intend to serve in my new restaurant will be out of your league. But as I said, I'm sure I can find enough work to keep you occupied.'

Jessamy opened and closed her mouth in impotent rage. Out of her league! How dared he? Did he think he was going to get a top London chef to come and cook for him in this out-of-the-way place? And to tell her he'd find enough work to keep her occupied! For all the world as if she was a child to be kept out of mischief.

As she stood there vainly searching for something withering to retort, Barry tugged at her arm. 'Jess, I think it's time you started to think about lunch. You will be staying, Mr Monro?'

The new owner inclined his head courteously. 'Thank you. But don't go to any trouble.' He looked at Jessamy. 'I'll make do with what you usually serve the customers.'

'Then if you'll excuse us just a moment ...' Barry almost dragged Jessamy out of the office and down the passage to the kitchen where they would be out of earshot.

'Jess, for heaven's sake!' He almost shook her in

exasperation. 'I've gone to a lot of trouble to pave the way for you, telling him how talented and willing you are, and now you're doing your best to wreck all my groundwork. Do you *want* to go back on the dole again?'

She shook her head. 'Of course I don't, but—'

'Well, the way you're talking to Monro, you soon will be. It's no skin off his nose whether he takes you on the payroll or not. So why not calm down a bit and be grateful he hasn't already thrown you out on your neck?'

'Grateful!' Jessamy exploded with indignation. 'I should *thank* him for reducing me to a skivvy when I know perfectly well I'm capable of taking over his new kitchens?'

'Well, here's your chance to show him. I mean . . .' He looked her up and down, grinning, 'you *do* look about sixteen in that outfit. You can't really blame Monro for not believing you're as good as you say you are.' His grin faded and he gripped her shoulders, his face earnest. 'So why not pull out all the stops with this lunch, eh? Serve up something that'll really make him take notice. I know you can do it.'

'I know what I'd like to give him,' she muttered darkly. 'Arsenic!'

'Yes, well . . .' His mouth twisted into a wry smile. 'But that wouldn't get me the marina back, would it?'

No. Nothing would undo the harm Luke Monro's chicanery had done to Barry. Her revulsion at such underhand and unscrupulous practices rose up in her again like a corrosive acid.

She burst out, 'Barry, I don't know how you can bear to go on working for him after what he did to you. Why, he practically stole your business from you!'

'Beggars can't be choosers,' he said heavily, his blue eyes bleak. 'I don't like the man and I certainly wouldn't trust him out of spitting distance, but what's the alternative to taking his job? I'm a good mechanic, but there are plenty of good mechanics on the dole. I'm trying to look on the bright side. I'll be drawing regular money whether the business is paying or not. Those worries will be Luke Monro's.'

And Jessamy hoped they would be considerable. She could see Barry's point of view. But it made her want to weep to see him so eager to accept a subservient position in the business he'd once owned. And subservient to the man who through pure greed had tricked him out of that business.

Well, Barry might be prepared to accept crumbs from Luke Monro's table, but she didn't think she could do it herself. The thought of having to come into regular contact with that hateful man, of having to take orders from him and not to be able to retaliate to his cutting remarks, of having to pretend respect when she could only despise him, was abhorrent to her. The very idea of having to be anywhere near him made her squirm as if she was wearing a hair shirt beneath her pink dungarees.

'I'm sorry, Barry, but I think I'd rather go back on the dole than work for Luke Monro.' It was a gut reaction, but even as she said it, cold common sense began to assert itself. Working for Barry she had earned very little over and above her board and her savings account was bare. She had enough money for her train fare to London, but she couldn't find the month's rent in advance any landlady would demand for even the humblest bedsitter. And it wasn't as if there was anyone who could help her. She had lost contact with the friends she'd made at college and all the family she had – her mother and her brother and sister-in-law – were on the other side of the world.

'Oh, don't say that, Jess.' Barry broke into her scurrying thoughts. 'Having you still working here is the only thing that would make it bearable for me.' She hesitated and he pressed his advantage. 'Please, Jess! At least give it a try. It might not be so bad.'

But it would be. She knew in her bones it would. 'All right, I'll give it a try,' she conceded reluctantly, then lifting her small chin, 'And if Luke Monro demands proof that I can cook a meal as good as any he's eaten anywhere in the world, then he'll get it!'

'That's my girl!' Barry plonked an approving kiss on the top of her head and hurried back to their big white chief.

Jessamy started at once to work out a menu. She longed for a nice juicy fillet of beef so she could nonchalantly serve up Beef Wellington in a melting crust or a succulent Beef Chasseur in a demi-glaze sauce. But she knew her deep-freeze didn't hold such a luxury.

Still, there were some chickens and luckily she'd taken one out of the freezer last night to defrost. French herbed chicken . . . that should titillate his tastebuds, with the herbed butter carefully inserted between the chicken breast and the skin. Served with . . . yes, potato scallops, crisp and golden on the outside and light and floury inside, new young buttered carrots spiked with the zest of an orange and her speciality, some of Joe Sutherland's tender young courgettes baked in a creamy egg custard.

Hardboiled eggs and prawns in a béchamel sauce for starters, she decided, and though she was tempted to try something like a Dacquoise for dessert, she reluctantly decided to settle for oranges in caramel.

Her rancour against Luke Monro slipped to the back of her mind as she worked, enjoying for the first time since she'd come to the marina the chance to let her imagination and her skills off the rein. She even grudgingly decided it might be worth humbling herself a little to Luke Monro if only he would give her the chance to cook like this all the time, but then she felt guilty because that was disloyal to Barry.

When she had the lunch under way Jessamy put a Closed sign on the door of the lounge bar and took trouble to set one of the larger tables attractively. Any casual customers would have to use the other bar, and for once she hoped there wouldn't be many demanding attention.

Luke Monro's assumption that she was a mere schoolgirl stung, and when everything was ready to serve she found time to slip back to her houseboat to change, dropping the pink dungarees and shirt at her feet and wriggling into a cornflower blue dress that swirled femininely round her hips and hugged her tiny waist, a blue that exactly matched her eyes.

She hesitated over make-up. She didn't often use it and was afraid of making a mess if she tried to hurry. Her cheeks were already glowing from her efforts in the kitchen, so she settled for a dash of lipstick and a dab of powder to take away the shine on her nose. Quickly pulling down the ponytail, she brushed her fair hair to bring out the glints, then tied it into a loose and much more sophisticated knot at the back of her neck.

'So I have an exclusive dining room,' Luke Monro commented as she led him to his table.

'I thought you'd expect to be private,' Jessamy said stiffly, thinking she could detect criticism in his tone. 'Any customers can use the other bar.'

He surveyed the table she had prepared, his expression giving nothing away. 'But not so private that I have to eat alone. Barry, won't you join me? That's if you've cooked enough for two?' he added to Jessamy as an afterthought.

'Of course.' She gritted her teeth and set another place. 'I just didn't expect you would want to eat with the staff,' she said with false sweetness.

His eyes glinted a danger signal. 'Get on with serving the food if you don't want a spanking, young woman!'

Her cheeks bearing two red flags of indignant colour

at his casual familiarity, Jessamy would dearly have liked to tip the contents of the iced water jug over his head.

Barry gave her an undercover thumbs-up sign when she cleared away their first course and she began to feel everything was going well. She even caught Luke Monro out in an appreciative sniff as she brought in the steaming, fragrant chicken and began to carve. And then the bell rang from the other bar, signalling the arrival of a customer demanding service.

Jessamy dithered. What was she expected to do now? Leave the chicken to get cold? She carved another slice off the breast, trying to hurry. The bell rang again, impatiently.

'Don't you think you ought to attend to the paying customers?' Luke Monro was sitting back in his chair enjoying her dilemma.

'I'll see to the bar.' Barry had half risen from his seat when he was told sharply to sit down.

Luke got up himself and reached to take the carving knife and fork from her. So unwilling was she to have him touch her, she snatched her hands away and the knife clattered on to the table between them.

Only too glad to escape, she scuttled through to the other bar to serve lager and a ploughman's lunch of crusty bread and her home-made pâté to the couple who were waiting. Another group came in who couldn't make up their minds between a similar ploughman's lunch or a slice of her prawn quiche and salad, and by the time she got back to her lunch table the two men were well into their meal, but so deep in conversation that Luke Monro at least didn't appear to know or care what he was eating.

So much for Barry's idea of proving her skill, she thought crossly. All she'd proved was how flustered she could get when two things demanded her attention at once.

Not by so much as a flicker did Luke Monro show appreciation or even acknowledge her existence as she cleared away the empty plates and set the oranges in caramel before him, and those dishes too were cleared away without any comment forthcoming.

At last she could stand it no longer. She would force the ill-mannered brute to admit she knew what she was doing in the kitchen. 'Was your lunch to your liking . . . sir?' she asked, passing his coffee cup.

'Not bad . . .' He took a sip of coffee, then for the first time since he had sat down at the table he looked directly at her over the rim of his cup.

Her cheeks began to burn, for from the knowing expression in his dark eyes she could see he was very much aware of how hard she had been trying to impress. And not only with her culinary skill either, she realised as his glance lingered over her breasts thrusting at the tight bodice of her blue dress.

## CHAPTER TWO

'THAT was some meal, Jess!' Barry came up behind her to give her an encouraging pat on the back as she stood at the kitchen sink, labouring over the washing up. He looked much more familiar now, she noted, having taken off the business suit that had sat so uncomfortably on him and returned to his usual tee-shirt and jeans. 'I'm sure Mr Monro thought so too,' he added.

'Because he said it wasn't bad?' Jessamy was still smarting from the faint praise that had been Luke Monro's only comment on her morning's efforts, and still fulminating at the blatant way he had stripped her with his eyes, as if he imagined he'd bought *her* along with the marina.

'Oh, come on ...' Barry coaxed. 'He didn't leave anything on his plate, did he? He's just not the kind of man to go into raptures over anything, and let's face it, you had been doing your best to put his back up this morning. But I reckon that showed him, love. I don't think there's much doubt he'll be letting you run his new restaurant kitchen.'

Jessamy only wished she felt half as confident. In fact she was sure that even if she cooked as well as any top chef in London, Luke Monro still wouldn't trust her with the job. Having already made up his mind such a job would be beyond her, he wasn't the type to back down and admit he was wrong.

'Where is he now?' she asked. 'I suppose it's too much to hope he's gone back to London?'

'Only as far as Market Swinford,' Barry grinned. 'He's gone to see Frazer, the builder, about setting a date to start all the alterations.'

'Already?' Jessamy stared at him. 'But he can't start knocking this place about just like that! Doesn't Mr High and Mighty Monro realise he'll need planning permission from the Council?'

'He's already got that.'

'But he can't have!' She laughed in disbelief. 'He only bought the place yesterday, and getting plans passed takes months ... well, weeks anyway.'

'He bought my business yesterday,' Barry corrected her. 'You forget, he actually bought the property from my previous landlord over twelve months ago.' Bitterness crept back into his voice again. 'By the time he dropped the bombshell that he wasn't renewing my lease, he already had the local planning department in his pocket.'

'So there's nothing to stop him tearing the place apart tomorrow!' Jessamy was deeply shaken. She had been assuming things would go on as usual for a while at least. She had been telling herself she would have a few weeks to get used to the idea of working for a man who not only had the unfortunate knack of making her hackles rise every time she crossed his path, but a man whose lack of principles she despised. Maybe it wasn't actually illegal, the way he had wrested the marina out of Barry's hands, but no one would ever persuade her it was honest.

'The sooner he starts to get things moving, the better I'll be pleased,' Barry said surprisingly.

'You mean you don't mind that he's going to start doing all the things you planned to do?' She really couldn't understand how Barry could take all this lying down. If Luke Monro had done to her what he'd done to Barry, she would have felt like setting fire to the place rather than let him reap any benefit.

'Use your head, Jess!' Leaning against the draining board beside her, he punched her shoulder playfully. 'Monro's a businessman with fingers in all sorts of pies. Once he's stirred things up a bit round here he's going to disappear back to London and leave us to get on with running things our own way.'

She looked at him doubtfully. Of course Barry must know Luke Monro much better than she did, but their new boss didn't strike *her* as the sort of man who would allow anyone to run any enterprise of his any way but *his* way.

She put the last dish on the drainer and wiped round the sink. 'All I hope is that a large dishwasher will be one of his first improvements,' she said fervently.

'I'll make sure it's high on the list of priorities,' Barry boasted. 'I tell you, Jess, a rich man like Monro . . . he's like a kid with a new toy. He'll soon get tired of it. You don't expect him to get his hands dirty, do you? He's not going to rough it around here keeping an eye on things. He'll be off back to that penthouse of his in London while we do all the work.'

Just how far out Barry was in his estimation began to

become apparent later that afternoon. As Jessamy crossed the bridge back to her houseboat for a well earned rest before the inn opened again to catch the evening trade, she noticed the distinctive cream car was parked near the boatyard. No doubt its owner was chivvying the mechanics now, she thought sourly. But she was wrong. No sooner had she set foot on her boat than his head appeared at her doorway.

All Barry's warnings about guarding her tongue were forgotten at this blatant invasion of her privacy. 'I know you own all this now,' she said with withering fury, 'but usually even a landlord waits to be invited before making free with someone's home!'

'*You* live here?'

'Don't pretend to sound surprised,' she snapped. 'Is there any reason why I shouldn't?'

'No, of course not. I just assumed ...' His voice trailed off.

'You assumed what? That I constituted a hazard to other road users cycling back to the village every night?' The well deck of the boat was small, and her skin prickled with discomfort at being forced into such close proximity with him.

'No, I assumed you lived up at the inn with Barry,' he said bluntly.

Jessamy's face flamed. 'I think you should explain that unwarranted assumption!'

He shrugged. 'Well, the pair of you do put up a concerted front, Barry pushing your talents for all he's worth and you leaping to his defence if I have the temerity to criticise him. And in this day and age ...' His implication that they must be sharing the same bed was unmistakable.

'Oh, I'm sure in your circle no one would raise an eyebrow.' She was shaking with indignation. 'I don't happen to have such alleycat morals. I prefer to wait till I'm married before I move in with a man.'

There was a sardonic gleam in his dark eyes, which were a very dark grey and not black as she'd first thought. 'And Barry's dragging his feet? No ...' He held up his hands as if to ward off a blow. 'I'm sorry, I shouldn't have said that. It's none of my business anyway.'

'No, it isn't.' Jessamy took several deep breaths to calm herself down after his outrageously impertinent suggestion. 'Is there something I can do for you, Mr Monro?' she said pointedly as he was still blocking the entrance to her houseboat. 'I was just going to have a few minutes' rest.'

'Yes, you can show me round your boat if you will. I'd only quite literally poked my head in the door when you arrived.' He grinned wickedly. 'I wouldn't have had time to burgle your family heirlooms even if I'd wanted to!'

Every instinct rebelled at the idea of having this man inside her home, but she supposed that as he now owned every stick of it, she couldn't reasonably refuse his request. Neither did she enjoy being reminded what a fool she'd made of herself that morning mistaking him for a sneak-thief.

'What else was I to think?' she said sharply as she led the way into the main saloon of the houseboat that doubled as her sitting and dining room, keeping as much space between them as possible. 'I'd seen your car hidden in the bushes at the side of the road, and then finding you apparently searching the office ...'

'Hidden in the bushes?' His eyebrows soared. 'I assure you all I was concerned about was getting the car well off the road.' His lips twitched. 'Out of the way of girls on bicycles.'

'But why not drive right up to the marina?' she demanded, ignoring his taunt. 'Like any bona fide visitor?'

'Because, my dear Miss Daunay, I wanted to get a

good look at the state of that track.' He suddenly sounded bored with the whole subject. 'It'll have to be made into a proper road to take all the traffic I hope the marina will attract by the time the improvements are finished.'

He had an answer for everything. Jessamy felt the hot colour burning her cheeks again and cursed the fair skin that betrayed her discomfiture so readily. But though it went against the grain to apologise, she supposed she owed it to him. 'I'm sorry,' she muttered.

'And I'm sorry too,' he said surprisingly with a smile that softened the hard planes of his face. 'Look, can't we forget our unfortunate meeting and begin again?'

Jessamy had always thought of her boat as roomy, but it seemed suddenly to have shrunk. Luke Monro filled it with his presence, his head bent a little towards her to clear the low roof, his deep-set grey eyes boring into her steadily, waiting for an answer.

Every nerve end quivered with awareness as she stared up into that darkly handsome face. The breeze had blown a lock of black hair forward on to his brow, breaking the line of the widow's peak. For the first time she noticed a small cleft in his chin, and on the bridge of his nose a tiny bump and a faint, crescent-shaped scar, as if he might have made contact with a cricket ball as a boy, or fallen out of a tree, perhaps.

Shaking herself to dissipate that disturbing mental image, she moved abruptly away from him. She supposed even a man as ruthless and unprincipled as Luke Monro had shown himself to be must have been a child once, and probably a spoilt one at that, she told herself sourly, so she needn't let it get to her. And what nefarious scheme was he cooking up now, turning on his not inconsiderable charm and wheedling her into accepting his olive branch? It wasn't because he liked the colour of her eyes, that was for sure. A man who could force Barry out of business with such ruthless disregard for fairness and decency didn't do anything without a very good reason, and she was darned if she was going to let him charm her into forgetting that.

'I'm afraid I don't know what you mean, Mr Monro,' she said coldly. 'We *have* met, and not even you can put the clock back.'

'Have it your own way, Miss Daunay.' His voice was equally cold. 'Now, you were going to show me round the boat.'

She was quick to notice he didn't say *'your'* boat, but then he wouldn't would he? It was *his* boat and would only remain her home at his whim. The instinctive distaste at having him here at all rose up in her again.

'This, as you can see, is the main saloon,' she said woodenly. 'And this . . .' she passed quickly through the door at the far end, '. . . is the galley. Cooker and refrigerator run off bottled gas, but the lighting is electric, wired from the mains at the inn. Oh, and water is pumped from the fresh water tanks.' She rattled off the main features like a machinegun. She might be obliged to accord him this tour, but she didn't see why it should be leisurely.

Through the galley she opened the first door along the narrow passageway. 'The shower and "usual offices".' She would have closed the door again immediately, allowing him only the briefest glimpse, but he put out his hand to prevent her, his arm brushing against her breasts. It was only the lightest of accidental contact, but she jerked away as if it had been a deliberate assault. She couldn't logically account for this new emotion that was making her breathing come raggedly. She didn't like the man at all. She couldn't forgive or forget what he had done to Barry and she bitterly resented his intrusion into their lives, but that was no reason that he should provoke what she recognised as pure fright.

'How do you heat the water?' he asked, either not

noticing, or choosing to ignore her instinctive recoil from his touch.

'The—the woodburning stove in the saloon has a back boiler,' she stuttered, struggling to get herself under control again. 'But it makes the place too hot in summer, so I make do with cold showers.'

'Subduing the flesh?'

She glanced up into his face, wide-eyed and uncertain what he meant, until she met the unmistakable mockery in his eyes. Her cheeks scorched. He was telling her he *had* noticed the profoundly disturbing effect he had on her, and he was thoroughly enjoying her discomfiture!

She moved quickly down the passage, flinging open the next door and this time standing well back. 'The spare cabin,' she said baldly, intending to add nothing more, but then realising there was only one more door to open for him, the double berth cabin at the end of the passage she used herself, and the idea of taking this man into her bedroom filled her with repugnance and embarrassment. A bedroom was very personal, telling any stranger who entered it a lot about the occupant.

To postpone that revealing moment she went on hurriedly, 'Of course the spare cabin's a bit sparse, but I've never had occasion to use it yet. New curtains and bedcover and a few pictures and ornaments about would make a different place of it.'

But now Jessamy was willing for him to examine the cabin more closely, he seemed to have lost interest. He pulled the door shut, but Jessamy made no move to continue the tour. She could see the door of her own cabin was ajar and lying in a heap on the floor were the pink dungarees she had discarded so hastily earlier in the day.

'And that has to be your bedroom.' He nodded towards the half open door.

Still Jessamy didn't offer to show him. 'I suppose

you're going to insist on seeing in there too,' she said bitterly.

'I haven't *insisted* on anything yet,' he said in a voice as smooth as silk. 'I asked if you might show me round and you very hospitably agreed.'

Jessamy remained silent, though privately she thought he had a great capacity for self-delusion if he really believed that.

'You can relax.' His voice had a light, mocking tone now. 'I don't intend to invade your virginal privacy—unless I'm invited.'

And *that* would never happen. She scurried back along the passage to the saloon. Silly to feel so weak with relief, but it was as if an order to strip in front of this man had at the last moment been rescinded. Perhaps now he would go and leave her in peace to enjoy what was left of her afternoon siesta.

But he didn't seem in any hurry. 'It's all surprisingly cosy,' he commented, looking round the saloon again.

'I think so. I love it.' Jessamy was unaware of the glow of pride in her face as she glanced around at some of the touches that were all her own; the curtains and cushions, a few favourite pictures, her books and the house plant she had nurtured from a very unpromising beginning. This was an Easter cactus, still a mass of exotic orange blooms standing in the middle of the table, a bright splash of colour against the soft moss greens she had chosen for the curtains and cushions.

A smile hovered round his mouth and warmed his grey eyes. 'You don't find it too quiet here? Don't you ever hanker after the excitement of the big city?'

'No.' Her response was immediate and definite. 'It's all right for people like you who can afford a nice home in one of the more glamorous and accessible districts and still be able to afford to go to theatres and restaurants.' She eyed those heavy gold cuff-links peeping from the sleeves of his expensive suit and thought it was time someone told him what the real world was like. 'For someone like me there's precious little excitement living in a grotty bedsitter with all your cash going on bus and tube fares. I know. I had months and months on the dole after I left college, before Barry gave me this job. Believe me, it's like paradise here after that.'

'But what do you do in your spare time?' he asked curiously. 'I notice there's not even a cinema in Market Swinford.'

She couldn't help a superior smile at the man's ignorance. 'My problem's not how to fill my spare time but to find enough spare time to join in all the activities that go on around here.'

'Such as?' he prompted.

'For a start, there's a film club that meets once a fortnight in the community centre at the school, so we get to see most of the films worth seeing. Then there's the village drama group. They put on plays three times a year *and* a pantomime at Christmas. And hardly a week goes by without someone holding a dance in the village hall to raise money for one local cause or another. There are church social evenings, not to mention parties in people's houses, and there must be at least a dozen organisations you can join, from the Young Farmers' Club to the Women's Institute. And——'

'Stop . . . stop!' he protested, laughing. 'I'll take your word for it that there's a seething anthill beneath the sleepy front the village puts up. No wonder you don't miss the city when you live such a life of riotous dissipation!'

'I don't know about dissipation, but it can certainly be riotous.' Jessamy found herself smiling reminiscently as she thought of some of the hilarious evenings she'd spent with the friendly villagers.

With an abrupt change of subject, Luke Monro

jerked his head to indicate the other houseboat moored beyond her bows. 'Who's your neighbour?'

'No one at present. One of the mechanics lived in it, but when he got married a couple of months ago his girl insisted on a flat in Market Swinford. She said *she* wasn't going to bury herself in the back of beyond.' Jessamy's voice betrayed the fact that she found such an attitude incomprehensible.

'So it's empty?' he said thoughtfully. 'Mind if we take a look?'

'I suppose not, but . . .' She frowned, shrugging. 'It's very much the same as this one.'

'I'd still like to see it,' he insisted.

Jessamy recognised an order when she heard one. So much for her rest period, she thought resentfully as she walked away from him into the galley.

'I suppose Barry has the key?' he called after her.

'No, I do, as I'm the one who has to go in from time to time to dust and air the place.' She walked back into the saloon, the key in her hand, and couldn't resist adding sarcastically, 'So if you're thinking of moving in, it should be more or less habitable.'

'I was thinking exactly that,' he said.

'You can't be serious!' Astonishment stopped her dead in her tracks so he cannoned into her.

'Can't I?' He gripped her shoulders to steady her and she found herself pressed against his broad chest, his face only inches from hers. It was as if someone had put an electric charge through her, making every nerve end quiver and tingle, an electric charge that short-circuited her powers of speech so that she opened and closed her mouth soundlessly.

'It strikes me it would make an eminently suitable base,' said Luke Monro, his eyes mirroring the amusement he apparently felt at her goggling incoherence before he finally released her.

Jessamy moved then, making a shaky progress off the boat and along the towpath.

'I don't flatter myself I have your home-making skills,' he said, following her. 'But I can't do worse than that hotel in Market Swinford I booked into. Besides, it'll be much more convenient living right on the spot.'

'You're not going back to London, then? Barry thought you'd only be popping over here now and again to see how things were going.' As soon as she'd said it, Jessamy realised her mistake.

'Barry has a lot to learn about the way I operate,' he said grimly, his eyes like chips of ice.

As Jessamy unlocked the door of the empty houseboat she was met by a wall of hot, stale air, and she was glad to be able to cover her embarrassment by rushing round opening all the windows.

'It'll soon freshen up,' she said, but he didn't seem to hear her. He was prowling about examining all the fittings.

'The shower doesn't seem to work,' he said.

'No, the fresh water tank will need filling.'

'Does it take long?'

'About ten minutes or so. There's a standpipe by the bridge connected to the water mains and a hose in the locker out on the well deck. I can do it in the morning when I refill my tank, if you like.'

'If you show me where everything is, I'll do it now. I do like a shower first thing in the morning.'

Jessamy stared at him. 'You're not sleeping here tonight!' Her voice squeaked in surprise.

'I wish you wouldn't keep telling me what I'm *not* going to do.' There was a gleam in his eyes she didn't quite know what to make of.

'B—but you said yourself you're booked into a hotel in Market Swinford,' she stuttered.

'As long as I pay for the room I don't think it's obligatory to actually sleep in it.' One of those sardonic eyebrows rose mockingly as he asked, 'Now are there any more reasons why I can't move in here tonight?'

'No—no, I suppose not,' Jessamy said faintly, trying to collect her scattered wits and think what needed to be done. 'Things like milk and tea and coffee I can fetch from the stores at the inn. Oh, and you'll need a bottle of gas for the cooker and fridge. I'll get one of the mechanics to bring one over, and he can fill your water tank at the same time. And then there's your bed . . .'

She hurried through into the main cabin in the bows and felt the mattress all over.

'What on earth are you doing?' Luke Monro watched her from the doorway.

'Making sure it's not damp. I don't think it is, but I don't know about . . .' She wrenched open the locker beneath the bed and dragged out an armful of blankets, wrinkling her nose. 'They're a bit musty.'

Staggering under the weight, she would have pushed past him if he hadn't determinedly blocked her way. 'Now where are you going with those?'

'To air them, of course. There's still quite a lot of heat in the sun. If I spread them out on the roof of the boat for a while——'

Without warning he swept the bundle out of her arms. 'I know you firmly believe I live a sybaritic life of ease in London, waited on hand and foot, but I'm not absolutely helpless. And didn't you say something about this being your rest time?'

'Well, yes, but I thought——'

'Then go and rest. Heaven knows, you've earned it.' Burdened as he was with the blankets, he managed to shoo her back along the passage.

Irrationally Jessamy felt annoyed as she walked back to her own boat. Luke Monro was everything she hated in a man. He was overbearing and arrogant, callous and utterly unscrupulous. Even such a minor show of thoughtfulness didn't fit in with her picture of him at all.

She kicked off her sandals and stretched out on the divan in the saloon, watching the dancing reflections of sun on water playing on the roof over her head, listening drowsily to the voices of Luke Monro and the mechanic as they filled the water tank on his boat and connected up the new bottle of gas. And she wondered what Barry would make of the news that the man he confidently expected to be an absentee boss was actually going to be living on the premises.

'He's gone, then.' Barry watched from the window of the bar as Luke Monro's car roared away up the track to the road. 'Did he say when he'd be back?'

'In about half an hour, I should think,' Jessamy replied, setting out her bar snacks under their see-through covers. 'He's only gone back to the hotel to collect his luggage.' She'd learned that when she'd taken a few stores over to stock his galley just before she'd opened the bar. 'Didn't he tell you he's moved into the empty houseboat?'

'Moved in? You mean permanently?' One look at his face told her he hadn't known, and that as she'd expected, the news was most unwelcome.

'I don't know about permanently, but he certainly means to be on hand while all the alterations are going on,' she told him.

Barry swore softly under his breath. 'That's all we need, him under our feet all the time, cracking his whip and interfering!'

'Well, I was afraid you were being too optimistic, thinking he'd leave everything to us.' She began to polish the glasses.

'Why was he so keen for me to stay on, then?' Barry sounded aggrieved. 'He appointed me manager, so why doesn't he let me get on with managing?'

That surprised her. It was the first time she'd heard any mention of a manager's position.

'Haven't I already been running the place for years?' he asked.

She agreed he had, but she couldn't help thinking that Barry's idea of running the marina might be very different from Luke Monro's.

The trouble was that although Barry could talk boats to anyone, when it came to social chit-chat he wouldn't make the effort. He hadn't even bothered to change from the jeans and tee-shirt he'd been wearing all afternoon. She was sure it was the kind of thing Luke Monro would notice and comment on. And after all, there was more to running the marina than being a good mechanic.

'Perhaps now you're a manager you should try to look the part,' she suggested. 'I mean, dress up a bit when you're serving in the bar. Chat to the customers. It's all part of public relations.'

'Oh, leave off, Jess!' His face creased into an embarrassed grin. 'You'll be having me prancing about in a white tuxedo next!'

'When the new restaurant's open I wouldn't be at all surprised if Mr Monro doesn't insist you wear evening dress.' There was a note of exasperation in her voice at his expression of dismay. 'Well, you can hardly swan around asking the patrons if they're satisfied, wearing the same jeans and tee-shirt you've disembowelled a boat in.'

Luckily the first customers of the evening put a stop to the argument before it could get heated.

The warm, sunny evening brought a lot of people out for a walk along the canal and they were kept busy in the two bars serving long, cool drinks and Jessamy's bar snacks to satisfy thirst and appetites whipped up by fresh air and exercise. But by the time the fiery ball of the sun had sunk below the horizon, both bars had emptied as people left before it grew too dark to see the towpath.

Jessamy finished washing the glasses, cleared up the bars and went to the kitchen to take food from the freezer to defrost overnight ready to start cooking again in the morning. It was still only just after ten o'clock when she said goodnight to Barry and walked back to her boat.

Now the sun had gone down there was a distinct chill in the air, reminding her that summer hadn't really come yet. And the glow of light spilling on to the towpath from the windows of Luke Monro's houseboat did nothing to dispel her shivers. The idea of him sleeping only yards away was acutely disturbing.

Gooseflesh pimpling her arms she pushed open her door and switched on the light. But the familiar room carried the faint scent of his after shave and as she hurried through to the galley to put the kettle on for a hot drink it was as if those enigmatic eyes were still watching her.

If Luke Monro had an irresistible urge to play with boats, why couldn't it have been some other marina he'd fixed his greedy sights on? There must be many places far more glamorous than this that he could have made a bid for, without turning her and Barry's lives upside down.

She reached down a mug, irritably pushing a pile of clean linen out of the way, so some of it slid on to the floor. As she bent to pick it up she realised with a sinking feeling in the pit of her stomach that this was something she had forgotten when she'd been checking to see that Luke Monro's houseboat was fully equipped.

Well, let him sleep in rough blankets for once; the experience might be good for him, she thought, turning back to the kettle which was nearly boiling. She was paid to cook for him, not play chambermaid. And yet she found herself turning off the gas jet under the kettle and sorting out what would be needed from her pile of clean laundry. Her position at the marina depended now on her making a good impression on her new boss, however much the idea rankled, and perhaps it wouldn't be such a bad thing to show she could be efficient and conscientious.

A lazy voice called 'Come in', when she knocked on Luke Monro's door, and she obeyed, to find the strains of a Mozart piano concerto from a portable radio-cassette player filling the saloon and Luke Monro, wearing a towelling bathrobe, his dark hair damp and rumpled as if he'd just come from under the shower, reclining on the divan. He got up and switched off the music.

'I'm sorry.' All the nervous uncertainty that this man invariably roused in her made her prattle breathlessly, 'I'm interrupting you, and that was lovely. But I just remembered your boat isn't equipped with sheets and towels, so I've brought you some of mine. You can borrow them till you have time to go out and buy some.'

To her astonishment he started to laugh. 'Jessamy Daunay, you're priceless!' And at her bewildered expression he laughed even harder, falling back on the divan helplessly while she watched in growing anger. What had she said or done that was so funny?

'Oh, please, don't look like that.' He made an effort to control his hilarity. 'I'm sorry, but you're just like a mother hen running round after her chicks.'

Two flags of indignant colour burned in her cheeks and her eyes sparked with temper. 'First I'm a child and now I'm a mother hen!' she snapped. 'You're not very consistent, are you?'

He stopped laughing abruptly and stood up, towering over her in the confined space. 'And actually you're neither.' He took the pile of linen from her arms and dropped it on the table. 'You're a remarkably pretty young woman. Very appealing . . .'

She stood mesmerised as he reached for her shoulders, pulling her against him. His mouth came down on hers, at first with no more than a butterfly's touch, but at that first gently teasing contact something quite extraordinary happened. It was as if a bud that had been tightly closed inside her suddenly opened with a small explosion, releasing sensations and emotions she never realised she was capable of feeling. Without any conscious volition on her part, her arms reached up to circle his neck. Her body too seemed suddenly to have developed a life of its own, straining close to him, moulding her curves against his muscled hardness.

It was Luke who drew back first, the look in his deep set eyes unfathomable. 'Wow! For a girl who values her virginity, you certainly play with fire!'

His drawling voice brought her back to sanity more effectively than a douche of cold water. With a gasp she tore herself out of his restraining arms, her face scarlet with mortification.

'You—you beast! You unmitigated cad!'

The mouth that a moment ago had been tasting her sweetness tightened, the dark brows lowered and the deep-set eyes were as cold and hard as wet slate. 'If I'm a beast, what does that make you? Coming to my boat at this time of night on such a flimsy pretext. Don't try to pretend you didn't intend to be kissed, or that you didn't enjoy it!'

He was accusing her of coming here deliberately to make a pass at him! 'It—it wasn't like that!' she began in shocked indignation.

'Wasn't it?' With great deliberation he tightened the tie of his bathrobe which had fallen partially open, leaving no doubt at all that beneath it he was naked.

Scorching colour rose in a tide up her throat and flooded her cheeks. 'You—you conceited ape!' she spluttered in impotent fury. 'If you think I have the slightest interest in a man so entirely lacking in moral principles then you have a very over-inflated opinion of yourself!'

'We're getting quite a menagerie in here—a beast, an ape and a wildcat! If I misread your motives then I'm sorry.' But the tone of his voice told her he didn't really believe her protestations of innocence.

'You will be sorry before morning, sleeping in those scratchy blankets. I hope they bring you out in a very painful rash!' In one movement Jessamy gathered up the bedlinen she had offered to loan him and swept off his boat, slamming the door behind her.

Righteous indignation bolstered her until she got to bed, but as she lay there sleepless, the scene re-enacted itself over and over in her imagination and each time the part she had played in it seemed more and more shameful.

It wasn't as if she'd never been kissed before. She was twenty-three for heaven's sake. There had been several romances with fellow students while she'd been at college. But no man's kiss had ever stirred her as Luke's had done. No man had ever made her lose her head before, rousing in her such burning longings that sanity and reason were forgotten.

And the fact that it was a man she so thoroughly despised who had made her feel like that was doubly shaming.


CHAPTER THREE

ON Monday morning Jessamy was woken by the sound of a heavy lorry revving and a sudden rumble like thunder. She peered out of the houseboat window, but the belt of trees screened the activity that seemed to have erupted in their quiet backwater.

She dressed quickly and from the vantage point of the bridge saw an earth-mover stripping the turf from the field at the top of the track and a dumper truck tipping hardcore on to the bared earth, while two men with a tape measure drove in marking stakes, and she realised work had already begun on making the marina's new car park. And with the two men measuring up she instantly recognised the figure of Luke Monro directing operations. That V of dark hair coming down in a peak on his forehead was unmistakable even at a distance.

So he was back. The weekend's respite when he had taken himself off to London was over. She shivered, in spite of the warmth of the sun which was raising wreaths of mist off the wet grass after the weekend's rain.

Seeing her standing there on the bridge, he raised his hand in salute, but she turned away back to her boat, refusing to acknowledge his greeting.

'Jessamy!'

Pausing reluctantly at his call, she watched him coming towards her. Gone was the smart business suit. Instead he wore coffee-coloured slacks that hugged his narrow hips and a chunky sweater that emphasised the width of his shoulders, and the casual dress seemed to underline his male virility even more than his more formal attire had.

'You haven't wasted much time.' She nodded towards the busy workmen.

'The sooner this job is done, the sooner the builders can make a start without getting bogged down in the mud.' He looked down ruefully at his suede shoes darkened by the wet grass. 'It must have been raining here all weekend. At least it managed to stay dry in London, even if we didn't see the sun.'

'We', he'd said. Of course there would be plenty of pretty girls waiting to welcome him back to civilisation with open arms and reinforce his already overweening conceit.

Jessamy said coldly, 'Did you want me for something particular or just to pass the time of day?'

His friendly smile faded and his eyes hardened. 'For something particular. I want to see you and Barry in the office at ten o'clock. There's something important to discuss, so don't be late.' He turned on his heel and walked back to the workmen before she could open her mouth.

She found Barry in the repair shed happily tinkering with the engine of his own boat and gave him the message.

His face fell. 'Didn't you tell him the place is closed on Mondays, and it's the only time we get off in summer?'

'I didn't get the chance,' Jessamy protested. 'He just gave the order and marched off.'

Barry threw down his oily rag in disgust. 'Isn't that just great! He goes swanning off for the weekend, leaving us to slog our guts out for him, and then calmly cancels *our* time off!'

They were Jessamy's feelings exactly, though she didn't remember Barry doing much slogging over the weekend, at least not on their employer's behalf. He'd spent most of the time here in the repair shed playing with his boat, leaving her to run the inn alone.

'What does he want us for anyway?' Barry demanded.

She shrugged. 'He didn't take me into his confidence, just said it was important.'

'It had better be,' he said darkly. 'I know the first thing I intend to bring up—how often we can expect this sort of encroachment into our free time.'

Jessamy had intended to cycle the three miles into

Market Swinford to change her library books and had dressed casually in jeans and skinny rib sweater. Now, determined to present a strictly businesslike image, she returned to the boat to change, choosing the rather severely cut charcoal grey suit she had bought for the long, dispiriting round of job interviews she had undergone after leaving college, teaming it with a plain white shirt and medium-heeled black shoes. Scraping back her long fair hair and pinning it into a smooth coil on the crown of her head, she felt a picture of cool, unruffled efficiency.

Knowing the usual haphazard jumble in the office she got there early, and it was even worse than she remembered, box files stacked untidily on the floor instead of being replaced on their shelf, scraps of paper with scribbled notes strewing the desk, half made out bills lying about, some of them ringed with coffee stains.

By the time Barry slouched in, very disgruntled still at being dragged away from his precious boat, and Luke had followed briskly, carrying an important-looking briefcase, Jessamy had restored some order, clearing and polishing the desk, fetching two chairs from the bar and setting them for herself and Barry, and making sure there was a supply of paper and pencils in case they needed to take notes.

If either of the two men noticed the transformation, neither of them commented. Luke sat down at the desk and opened his briefcase. 'Thank you both for being here so promptly.'

'Especially as it's our day off,' Barry muttered sulkily.

Luke's eyebrows arched and Jessamy had to meet the full force of his coolly accusing eyes. 'Why didn't you tell me?'

'You didn't give me the chance,' she defended herself spiritedly.

His lips compressed but his voice was evenly controlled as he said, 'I'm sorry,' including them both in his apology. 'But if you'll bear with me ... this shouldn't take many minutes, but it does need to be settled.'

'Just as long as we know where we stand over time off,' Barry said doggedly.

'We'll come to that in a minute.' Luke was suppressing his irritation with obvious difficulty. 'We've settled your salary already, Barry, but Jessamy's . . .' He consulted a paper from his briefcase, then looked straight at her as he named a figure that took her breath away. 'If that's agreeable to you, of course.'

'Th—thank you . . .' she stuttered. 'I didn't expect anything like that.'

There was a satiric gleam in his eyes. 'Don't you think you're worth it?'

Her chin came up instantly. 'Yes. Yes, I do. I think I'm worth every penny.' She only wished such largesse didn't have to come from such a tainted source.

Instead of being put out by her spirited answer he actually looked mildly approving. 'Well, even with accommodation found, I don't know how you managed to live on the pittance you've been getting up to now.' His glance raked over her dark, severe suit and the corners of his mouth twitched as if he guessed her motive for wearing it. 'Go out and blow some of your windfall on something pretty.' His grin widened wolfishly. 'But I give you fair warning—I'll see you earn it!'

The hateful flush stained her cheeks again, but even as a frosty retort sprang to her lips, she saw him take a wad of crisp new banknotes from his briefcase and push them across the desk towards her.

'And this is your dress allowance, Jessamy. But there are definite strings attached.' He paused, as if deliberately courting the horrified suspicion that sprang into her mind.

The only dress allowance a cook would need was for overalls. Surely his insulting assumption that she'd been making a pass at him the other night hadn't led him to believe she would be willing to sell her favours in that direction!

But even as the appalling thought formed in her mind, Luke went on, 'I want it spent on two or three good dresses for evening. Nothing elaborate, mind. No sequins and lurex or way-out fashion. Elegant, understated dresses, something suitable for your duties as hostess on the hotel-boat.'

Jessamy's eyes had been boggling at the pile of money lying on the desk before her, but now her head snapped up and she stared at him in astonishment. 'Hotel-boat?'

Luke sat back in his chair. 'That's what I want to discuss with you both ... making this place into a centre for luxury cruises.'

'Well, of course we already hire out cruisers by the day,' Barry said importantly. 'So it's a logical step going in for bigger boats with living accommodation and hiring them out by the week. I'd thought of that one myself.'

But Luke shook his head. 'Not self-catering cruisers ... hotel-boats, with single and double berth cabins, showers, stateroom and bar, dining saloon, galley, running hot water and electricity. Luxury accommodation for up to eight people and a crew of two to run the boat and look after the passengers.'

'And you're going to run them from here ... on the canal?' Jessamy couldn't hide her incredulity.

He nodded. 'That's the idea. I hope as far as Stratford-on-Avon and back initially.'

Jessamy looked at Barry, but he obviously wasn't going to say anything, so it was up to her to give the *coup de grâce* and show Luke Monro he didn't know as much as he thought he did.

'To Stratford-on-Avon? And just how do you propose to get a cruiser that big—twelve foot six wide at least—through the seven-foot-wide locks?' Not for anything could she have kept the triumph out of her voice.

'Jessamy, I think you're going to be a real asset to this marina.' Luke was looking down at his hands and his voice was so silky smooth she blinked with surprise at this unexpected reaction to her demolition of his plan. Then he looked up at her, his eyes chillingly cold, and added in a voice with the cutting edge of steel, 'But *not* if you will insist on fighting me all the way.'

She felt withered by this onslaught and licked suddenly dry lips. 'I—I was only trying to point out——' she began, but he didn't let her finish.'

'No, you weren't. You were scoring off me and enjoying every moment. If you hope to continue working for me it's a habit you'll have to curb. Now, if you'll allow me to continue . . . Each floating hotel will consist of two narrow-boats, one towed behind the other. Plenty of room for guests and crew and still navigable through the locks.'

Under his ironic gaze Jessamy had never felt so small. And she supposed it did serve her right. She *had* been eager to score off him and she hadn't stopped to think, let alone ask questions.

'And Jess is to be hostess on one of these floating hotels?' Barry asked, looking as if he didn't like the sound of the idea.

So much for her hopes of taking over the kitchens in the new restaurant, a very chastened Jessamy thought as Luke nodded. Still, presumably she would be doing all the cooking on the boat as well as acting as hostess. It might even be rather fun. And it would mean, with all those miles between her and Luke Monro, she would have a measure of independence, free from the temptation to take him down a peg again and incur another blistering attack like the one she had just brought on herself.

'And I'd like you to be the other crew member, Barry,' said Luke. 'Actually in charge of the boat and all the passengers.'.

'Me?' Barry's face reddened with resentful shock. 'But I thought I was supposed to be helping run the marina, not puttering up and down the canal squiring a bunch of holidaymakers!'

Luke sighed. 'We'd get through all this a whole lot quicker if only you'd both be prepared to listen before you shoot me down in flames. The contractors have promised the car park and the new road will be finished by the end of the week, and then the builders will be moving in. Now they'll be able to get on a whole lot faster if we close the place down. It's not hygienic anyway, trying to serve food and drink with brick dust and plaster flying about, and we don't want inquisitive customers getting under the builders' feet and falling into trenches. So you see, Barry, there'll be nothing for you to do at the marina for quite a while.'

Barry grunted, unconvinced. 'What about the boat repair yard? You're not closing that, surely? We've got a fair bit of work booked in over the next few weeks.'

'No, I don't see that keeping the boatyard open will interfere with the building work,' Luke agreed. 'But you've got a couple of good mechanics there, and the older one . . . Ted, isn't it? . . . he strikes me as capable of taking charge while you're away.'

Barry's face reddened again in protest, but before he could voice his objections Luke went on smoothly, 'If you're going to work for me effectively, Barry, you're going to have to learn to delegate. The one-man-band days are over. And part of the job will be organising the hotel-boats and engaging and overseeing the crews to run them, so it's important that you have personal experience of what's needed.'

Barry subsided, obviously still disgruntled but at least willing to listen.

'This first trip will be something of a trial run,' Luke explained. 'You can work out the route on paper and estimate the time it'll take to get from one point to another, but you need to actually go over the ground yourself to establish regular bases for picking up fuel, fresh water and stores, to hunt out places of interest along the way for the guests to visit and to arrange transport to get them there if it's beyond walking distance.'

'But——' Jessamy began, then coloured up when Luke flicked a sardonic glance in her direction. 'I'm not trying to score off you again,' she insisted defensively, 'but it's May now. Haven't you left it a bit late to advertise this new venture? Most people will have booked their summer holidays by now.'

His smile still had a touch of frost at the edges. 'That's all taken care of. I have an interest in a travel agency business in London and they've already reported considerable interest in the idea among their clients. We'll only be running one pair of boats this season, and of course there won't be any paying guests on this first trip, just a handpicked bunch of friends who're willing to be guinea-pigs.'

'And what about the boats themselves?' Barry blustered. 'You're not going to pick up a pair ready equipped at the drop of a hat.'

'I already have,' Luke retorted calmly. 'They're ready for you to pick up in Birmingham as soon as you can get there, Barry.'

Once again it appeared that Luke Monro had thought of everything. But then, Jessamy reminded herself, the man who had planned the systematic take-over of Barry's marina wouldn't leave anything to chance. But what she wouldn't give to pierce that ruthlessly arrogant armour, to find his Achilles heel and watch him humbled!

He was lounging back in the chair behind the desk as comfortably as if he'd been occupying it for years instead of days, and those deep-set dark eyes were gazing straight at her, almost as if she had spoken her thoughts aloud and he was taunting her to do her worst. A tremor ran through her veins at that steady regard and she shifted in her chair, for some unfathomable reason thinking of the pressure of those well modelled lips on hers.

'When do we make this first trip, then?' she asked, and the more she thought about working on the boat far away from Luke Monro's disturbing presence, the more it appealed to her.

Luke looked at Barry. 'If you leave for Birmingham tomorrow, how long before you can have the boats here?'

Barry reached for a book off the shelf and did a few rapid calculations. 'Five . . . six days, I should think.'

'That's what I thought, so I've arranged for the guests to assemble here a week on Saturday. That'll give you, Jessamy, time to look after the more personal furnishings . . . bedding and towels, kitchen equipment and so on. I'm sure I don't have to spell it out.'

'I'll need help fetching the two boats from Birmingham,' Barry broke in quickly. 'Can't I take Jess?'

Luke frowned. 'I'd rather you didn't. There's going to be more than enough work for her here. Isn't there anyone else?'

'There's a likely lad in the village who's looking for a job,' Barry admitted reluctantly.

'Then use him. If he's any good we may make a regular crewman of him. Well, I think that just about wraps this meeting up, except . . .' Luke was about to close his briefcase when he paused and drew out a folded sheet of paper which he proceeded to spread out on top of the desk. 'You might like to take a look at the layout of the boats.'

They all leaned over the desk to look as Luke pointed out all the features. '*Tiger Lily* is the powered boat and has all the daytime facilities, the galley at the rear with the dining saloon next to it, a couple of W.C.s amidships and then the stateroom, where there's a small bar, leading out on to the well deck. On *Hyacinth*, the butty boat towed behind, more toilet facilities and showers, four single cabins and two twins, all with their own wardrobes and vanitory units with hot and cold water, and electric reading lamps. And of course, the crew's cabin.'

Jessamy stiffened. 'But there's only one cabin for the crew!'

'Yes—well, on the first trip there'll only be six guests, so you'll be able to use a guest cabin.' He straightened up, glancing across at her and then letting his gaze fall to the plan again. 'Of course, it would make it easier for any future trips if you two were married.'

'Married!' Barry's mouth had fallen open in astonishment while Jessamy's face whitened with shock and then flooded with colour.

She was remembering the day of Luke Monro's arrival and his entirely unwarranted assumption that because she and Barry had been working together at the marina for nine months without actually living together, it had to be because she was holding out for marriage while Barry was dragging his feet. So now he thought he'd step in and push things along, did he? For his own convenience, naturally. How *she* felt about it wouldn't concern him.

She rounded on him, her slight frame quivering with fury, her blue eyes flashing sparks. 'Just who do you think you are? God? If I ever decide I want a husband I'll find one for myself, thank you very much!'

If Jessamy hadn't been so angry she might have noticed that for the first time she had succeeded in ruffling Luke Monro's composure. He stood there staring at her in astonishment, as if wondering how on earth he'd managed to bring this hornets' nest down upon his head.

'How dare you try to run my life for me, you—you overbearing, conceited, selfish, money-grabbing boor?' she spluttered. 'If it's so important to you to squeeze in an extra fare-paying passenger, then you'd better find someone else to look after them!' She stormed blindly out of the office, slamming the door so hard the building shook.

Dashing the tears from her eyes with the back of her hand, she stumbled back to her boat and threw herself down on the divan, beating the cushion with her fists as if she wished it was Luke Monro's head, until at last, her furious energy spent, she just lay there feeling drained.

Well, she'd really done it now, she thought drearily as the last fizzing spark of her anger seeped away. She'd as good as given in her notice. And even if she hadn't made that final, fatal threat, there was no hope now of Luke Monro keeping her on here at the marina, not after all the names she'd called him. Only ten minutes before he'd been warning her she would be out if she continued to fight him.

She dragged herself dispiritedly off the divan and made her way down the boat to her bedroom. That was that, then. She had better start her packing, though she had no idea where she would go.

She pulled her suitcase from the locker beneath her bed and started to empty the drawers and wardrobe. And for some reason she was crying again, so she didn't hear the knock at the door. It wasn't until the dark figure looming suddenly in the doorway of her bedroom made her gasp that she realised she wasn't alone.

'You didn't answer when I knocked,' Luke Monro said.

She held the dressing gown she was folding

defensively to her chest, the tears drying on her cheeks. 'What do you want?'

'Would you believe . . . to apologise?'

She stared at him speechless, so sure had she been that his visit was only to make sure she would soon be off the premises.

'I still think you overreacted,' he added, 'but you were quite right. I had no business interfering in your private life.'

'Overreacted!' The spark of anger wasn't dead yet. 'When you'd just tried to marry me off to another employee as if you had some sort of *droit de seigneur*?'

His lips twitched. 'I don't think you quite mean that, do you?'

Jessamy stared at him blankly for a moment, then blushed to the roots of her hair, remembering that *droit de seigneur* was a feudal lord's right to spend the night before the wedding with any bride marrying on his estate.

Drawing her tattered dignity round her, she said, 'You know exactly what I mean.'

'Actually I thought I was doing you a favour,' he said ruefully.

'Then I hope you never want to do me an ill turn!' she flashed, but at the same time she couldn't help remembering she hadn't bothered to set the record straight when Luke had first jumped to the conclusion that she hoped to marry Barry if she could ever bring him to the point. She thought she'd better do it now.

'There's never been the slightest hint of romance between Barry and me,' she said. 'Barry's so wrapped up in the marina he'd run a mile at the very idea of marrying anyone. And as for me . . . I look on Barry as a friend, nothing more.'

Luke looked sceptical. 'Barry didn't give me that impression when I left him in the office just now. But as you so rightly point out, it's none of my business. I just want to assure you there'll be separate cabins for you both for as long as you're working the hotel-boats.'

Jessamy just stood there, puzzling so much over his first statement she hardly registered that he was offering the olive branch and telling her the job was still open.

'Jessamy, won't you please put all your things away again?' he said softly.

She blinked, looking up at him as his words sank in. 'You want me to stay?'

'I want you to stay.' He was looking at her with an expression that sent a tremor down her spine.

She had hardly restored all her belongings to their various drawers before she had another visitor. Barry walked straight in after only a perfunctory knock.

'I saw Monro coming over here,' he said without any preamble. 'What did he want? To give you your marching orders?'

'Actually he came to apologise.'

'It's more than you deserve, flying off at him like that.' But he looked pleased.

'Not at all,' she said sharply. 'He quite agreed that he should never have made such a preposterous suggestion.'

Barry prowled restlessly around the saloon, twitching at a curtain, picking up a book and putting it down again, twiddling a knob on her radio. 'Is it such a preposterous suggestion?' he burst out at last. 'Us getting married, I mean?'

She should have been prepared after Luke's hint, but she wasn't. Before she could stop herself she burst out laughing. 'You know as well as I do it's a non-starter, Barry.'

His face flushed a dull brick red and he looked hurt. 'Why is it?'

Jessamy wished she hadn't laughed. 'Because the idea would never have entered your head if Luke Monro hadn't put it there, and I'm darned if I'm marrying anyone to suit *his* convenience.'

'I don't agree,' Barry said doggedly. 'I'd have got around to it sooner or later.'

'But, Barry . . .' the urge to laugh was giving way to exasperation, 'you don't love me.'

'You don't know how I feel about you, Jess.' He put a clumsy hand on her arm. 'I'll admit while I had all the worry and responsibility of keeping the marina solvent I didn't have time for any fancy ideas. And in any case, I couldn't afford a wife then. But now . . . Monro's taken over all the headaches and I've got a regular income. I can afford to think about myself for a change . . . about *us*. We make a good team, you have to admit that.'

Oh, help! Jessamy thought. What mare's nest had Luke Monro started up here?

'No, I don't know how you feel,' she said gently, trying to make her move away from his touch not too blatant. 'But I know how *I* feel. I'm very fond of you, Barry. You're the best friend I've ever had. But I don't want to marry you. I don't love you.'

'It'll come, Jess.' He pursued her, grabbing her hands eagerly. 'I'll *make* you love me.' Before she could draw back he had gathered her roughly into his arms, his mouth coming down hard on hers.

At first she felt a terrible pity for him because she knew she was right. His kiss did nothing to stir her blood. It aroused no longing in her, prompted no ardour leaping to meet his. And then as his arms still imprisoned her and his big hands pawed her un-responsive body, anger began to rise in her.

'No, Barry.' She tore away from his possessive mouth and squirmed out of his arms. 'It's no good. You can't make me fall in love with you on demand.'

'Jess . . .' There was hurt in his eyes, bafflement across his blunt features.

'Barry . . . please!' She backed further away.

'Oh, all right!' Sulkily he slouched to the door. 'But I'm not giving up, you know. Not until you say yes.' He slammed the door behind him.

Jessamy sank on to the divan feeling suddenly weak and shaky, her hand going to her mouth as if to wipe away the imprint of Barry's lips. His unwelcome overtures couldn't have pointed up more sharply the difference in her reaction to his kiss, which had left her cold, and with even a mild feeling of distaste, and to Luke Monro's, which had set her on fire.

Not that she ever wanted to repeat the experience with Luke, she told herself hastily. She still felt shamed by her body's eager response to a man she could neither respect nor trust, a man she actively disliked.

The trouble was, putting a safe distance between herself and Luke Monro was going to throw her even more closely into Barry's company. It wasn't going to be easy to escape his unwelcome attentions cooped up with him on a boat.

It seemed she was trapped between the devil and the deep blue sea!

## CHAPTER FOUR

IT was a big relief to Jessamy when about ten o'clock the following morning Luke drove Barry and his crewman David into the city to catch the train for Birmingham to pick up the hotel-boats. Barry had made no more sudden lunges at her, thank goodness, but seemed to have decided the best way to ingratiate himself with her was to be helpful. She found his efforts anything but! He broke her best mixing bowl for a start, and then got in her way when she tried to clear up the broken glass.

When she'd bumped into him for the third time because he was hovering so close she couldn't stop herself saying crossly, 'Oh, for pity's sake, Barry! I've got work to do if you haven't.'

The look of hurt reproach he gave her made her feel uncomfortable. 'Shan't see you again for the best part of a week, Jess.'

'All I hope is in that time you'll have got this silly idea of marrying me out of your head,' she retorted, but he looked so miserable she was sorry for her waspish tone and transferred her irritation to Luke Monro. *He* was the one responsible for this harassment, putting the idea into Barry's head and turning a perfectly normal, often insensitive man into a lovesick calf.

As if called up by her resentful thoughts, Luke poked his head round the door and asked if Barry was ready.

'Yes, I'm coming.' Barry turned back to her pleadingly. 'Jess—you will think about it while I'm away, then?'

Just as if she hadn't spoken! Jessamy thought helplessly; as if she hadn't already told him it was no good. 'Barry—please!' She was uncomfortably aware of Luke watching and listening from the doorway.

But Barry wasn't to be put off. Like a thirsty man at a spring he grabbed her shoulders and crushed her mouth to his. She stood rigid in his embrace, hating Barry's persistence and hating the man watching the scene with sardonic detachment. When they'd gone she pounded the dough for the batch of bread she was baking and relieved her feelings by imagining she was pounding both their thick heads together.

After Barry's departure she managed to avoid Luke most of the time. He spent hours in the office working out costings or talking interminably on the telephone, and though he occasionally came into the bar in the evenings when she was serving, the weather had picked up again, so there were plenty of customers to occupy her attention with their outspoken comments as soon as they saw the notices she had posted warning of the temporary closure of the inn.

But early on Thursday afternoon, as she was putting the towel up on the beer pumps to indicate that it was closing time, he came into the bar. 'I think it's high time you and I did some shopping, Jessamy. The bedding and linens for the hotel-boats,' he reminded her as she looked at him blankly. 'I think duvets are going to be very much more labour-saving than blankets.'

She agreed, trying not to show her surprise that he should think of saving her work.

'So that's eight—no, ten duvets, counting two for the crew's quarters, covers for them, matching pillowslips and, if we can get them, matching towels. Do we have an account with a local wholesale supplier?'

'Well, we mostly use Hassell's in Market Swinford,' she said, 'but they're only a small firm and I doubt if they'll carry that many of one pattern in stock, not without ordering them specially, and that would take too long. But I'm almost sure Barry opened an account with Lambury's in the city, though we've never used it much. There should be a purchasing card in the office somewhere.'

'Right, the city it is. Go and powder your nose and put on a pretty dress while I hunt out this card.' As she walked past him to do his bidding he surprised her by slapping her bottom, pert in its tight blue jeans, then called after her cheerfully, 'I'll give you ten minutes, mind, no more!'

True to his word, as she rushed up breathlessly ten minutes later he was already revving the Jaguar. He leaned across and swung open the passenger door and she found herself sinking into the soft leather seat.

'Very pretty.' He glanced approvingly at the crisp burnt orange cotton dress she was wearing, then his glance went to her severely pinned up hair and he pulled a wry face. 'But why do you insist on trying to look like a schoolmarm? It doesn't suit you at all.' Before she realised what he had in mind he had whisked the pins out of her hair with a skill that spoke of long practice.

'That's better.' His hand lightly touched the silken tresses as they tumbled down over her shoulders. 'Such beautiful hair.'

Jessamy's face burned and for a few seconds she was powerless to drag her eyes away from his magnetic gaze. 'I—I have to keep it pinned up out of the way when I'm c—cooking,' she stuttered.

'But you're not in the kitchen now.' He leaned closer and Jessamy closed her eyes, her heart pounding like a steam hammer. But he didn't kiss her. He merely reached across for her seat-belt. Her eyes flew open again and she thought she saw amusement in his face as he fastened the belt around her, and then they were off, roaring away up the track, the force of the acceleration pushing her back in her seat.

She'd let him make a fool of her again, she thought furiously, her face burning even hotter as she silently castigated herself for allowing him to have this effect on her. She had to remind herself that that kiss the other night had meant nothing to him at all. So why had he done it? And why had he let her hair down just now with a look in his eyes that was almost tender?

Because he was a professional womaniser, she told herself scornfully. Flirting came as natural to him as breathing. If she was naïve and stupid enough to be taken in by his games then she deserved all she got.

Luke swung the car out of the track on to the road and they proceeded through the village at a decorous pace, but once they reached the main road he put his foot down and they fairly flew along. The sunshine roof was open and the breeze lifted and stirred Jessamy's loosened hair, and apart from the sound of rushing air there was barely any noise. She was amazed that a car of this vintage could purr along so smoothly and so effortlessly.

'This really is some car,' she remarked, running her fingers lightly over the satin-smooth walnut dashboard and down the leather door lining.

'You can say that again! There can't be a dozen like it left in the world, and none of those in such tip-top condition.' He sounded as proud as a small boy showing off a new toy. 'I spent about five years restoring it myself.'

'You're a mechanic?' She was quite unable to keep the surprise out of her voice, and she wondered if there was anything this man couldn't turn his hand to.

He grinned. 'Well, perhaps I ought to admit I also had expert help, a friend who's a mechanic on a racing car team. But I did some of the work myself.'

A reluctant laugh was forced out of her. 'Tell the truth and shame the devil! Still, Barry would be very interested. He loves playing with engines. He's doing a boat up himself.'

'Ah—Barry.' Luke's voice had lost its ebullience and was suddenly dry. 'He's a good mechanic?'

Remembering the embarrassing situation Luke had thrust her into with Barry she wished she hadn't brought up his name, but it was too late now. 'The best,' she said defensively, and it was just too bad if Luke got the wrong idea. She had to be honest and give Barry his due. 'No matter how clapped-out the engines of some of the boats that come into the yard seem, he always manages to get some more mileage out of them.'

He turned on the radio as if to dismiss that topic of conversation and a few minutes later was singing to a pop oldie, for all the world like someone released on an unexpected holiday and determined to enjoy it. He had a rather pleasing light baritone voice and before long Jessamy had been infected by his lightheartedness and was humming along with him.

The fifteen miles to the city were soon gobbled up. They parked the car and found Lambury's wholesale warehouse in a side street not far from the centre. Not only were they able to buy the bedding for the hotel-boats—the duvets and pillows, fitted sheets, slip covers and towels—but all the crockery, cutlery and glassware they would need too, not to mention equipment for the galley. The place was like an Aladdin's cave and Luke the genie with the lamp. Jessamy had only to suggest what was needed and it was added to the list of goods to be delivered later to the marina.

She was still bemused by this open-handed prodigality when they left the warehouse. 'I've never spent so much money in my whole life before,' she said, round-eyed, as they walked away.

'And you haven't finished yet,' Luke said cryptically, steering her down a street that seemed to be made up of the city's most expensive fashion shops. He stopped outside one that displayed a single exquisite gown in its window. 'I don't suppose you've done anything about those evening dresses I told you to buy, have you?'

She shook her head, the hated flush staining her cheeks again. In her fury at Luke's insulting suggestion that it would be more convenient for him if she and Barry were to marry, she had left the money he'd provided for the purpose lying on the desk in the office and she'd been too disturbed by Barry's reaction to the suggestion to think of it again.

'Then let's make that next on our agenda.' He made as if to go into the shop, but Jessamy stayed rooted to the spot.

'Here?' She cast a nervous glance at the superb creation in the window. 'It looks *much* too expensive!'

'Let me be the judge of that.' He took her arm and hustled her through the door.

Inside, the atmosphere was hushed and opulent. An impeccably dressed and coiffured saleswoman glided soundlesly forward over the thick carpet and enquired what she could show them. Jessamy was so overawed by it all she was struck dumb, and it was left to Luke to explain their needs.

They were seated on a dainty little sofa and while the saleswoman selected several garments from a glass-fronted rail, an acolyte produced as if by magic a tea tray which she set on a small table in front of them. Gown after gown was displayed before her, but Jessamy was too nervous of the eggshell-thin cup and saucer that was put into her hands to really take anything in. Again it was Luke who nodded at some and shook his head at others. And then the acolyte was relieving her of the cup and saucer, Luke was urging her to her feet and she was following the saleswoman into the fitting room.

The first dress to be slipped over her head was a shot silk of exactly the same sheeny mixture of blues and greens as she had seen on a kingfisher she had once been lucky enough to catch a glimpse of near her houseboat. She gasped at the sheer sensuous luxury of the pure silk against her skin.

'Oh, it's beautiful!' She ran her hand lingeringly over the full skirt and noticed how the colour seemed to make her eyes look more green than blue.

The saleswoman smiled and swished back the curtain. 'I'm sure the gentleman will think so.'

Jessamy hung back, suddenly shy as she realised she was expected to parade herself before Luke. She had to tell herself these were working clothes. Luke was footing the bill and so had every right to approve her choice. In the end she erupted from the changing room in a little rush, her cheeks burning with embarrassment.

'It's silk!' she told him breathlessly, holding a bunch of her skirt out for his inspection. 'Pure silk!'

She saw that tell-tale twitch of his lips and her cheeks burned brighter still as she wished she didn't betray her ingenuousness every time she opened her mouth, especially as he seemed very much at home in this overpoweringly feminine place, so much so that she wondered how many times he had done this before, and for how many other women.

'Let's see how it moves on you.' He twirled her away from him and she selfconsciously walked up and down in front of him. 'Yes, that's a definite possibility,' he said approvingly.

The next gown was a long-sleeved black wool, a wool so fine it was almost transparent, and the folds clung to her curves as if they were molten, the unrelieved black giving her skin a pearly creaminess and adding a new sheen to her fair hair. It was so very plain and simple there seemed nothing to it, but so superbly cut it seemed to change her into a different person. She could hardly take her eyes off her mirror image—that suddenly sophisticated and self-possessed young woman who looked back at her so coolly.

This time she left the fitting room with far less nervousness, discovering for the first time the self-assurance the perfect dress could lend. Not even the sudden widening of Luke's eyes or the way he straightened up in his seat as he caught sight of her ruffled her aplomb, for of course she knew it was the dress and not *her* that was the cause of his approval.

The changes went on. Some of the dresses Jessamy fell in love with on sight, others she knew did nothing for her, and usually Luke's reaction to them coincided with her own. Only once did they differ, over a floating floral chiffon that Jessamy thought ultra-feminine but Luke shook his head at. 'It extinguishes you, Jessamy, calls too much attention to itself. I see only the dress and not the girl inside it.'

She was disappointed but accepted his verdict, especially as the next dress she tried on was a bronze silk jersey that clung to her figure like a second skin and rippled with translucent colour as she moved.

The thing that really bothered her as she slipped from one gorgeous creation into another was that she could see no price tickets, only a tiny label stuck on to each hanger bearing a few undecipherable letters. But she knew from the superb cut and the fabulous fabrics that they must all be wickedly expensive.

At last she had tried on every dress that Luke had picked out and was dressed again in her own unremarkable burnt orange cotton. He rose easily from the sofa, taking out his cheque book. 'I think the black wool, the kingfisher silk and that bronze thing, don't you?' he said.

'Three? But you haven't even asked how much they are!' she hissed as the saleswoman began folding the ones he'd selected in tissue paper without turning a hair.

'You don't like them?' His dark eyebrows arched.

'You know I do. They're the most beautiful clothes I've ever seen, but——'

'Then it doesn't matter what they cost,' he said imperturbably.

But Jessamy couldn't feel happy about it. There was enough of the puritan in her make-up to make her feel deeply uncomfortable about a man buying her clothes, even when it was a purely business arrangement. Almost as if he knew what was going through her mind Luke said with all his old arrogance, 'Would it help if I told you to allow me to know my own business best?'

Jessamy flushed, but though she said nothing, she was thinking that even though she would be putting miles between herself and Luke Monro in a little over a week's time, she knew on every occasion she had to wear these clothes she would be reminded of him uncomfortably.

Luke insisted on carrying the large dress box the

gowns had been packed into, but they hadn't gone far down the street when he caught her arm, forcing her to a standstill outside an extremely chic shoe shop. 'Dresses like these need the right accessories,' he said. 'Why don't you get some shoes too while you're here?'

But Jessamy had had enough embarrassment for one day. 'I have plenty of shoes to be going on with, thank you,' she said firmly. 'Besides, there isn't time. If we don't go back right away I'm going to be late opening up the bar.'

He didn't argue, but when they'd reached the car and he'd stowed the dress box safely in the trunk and handed her into the passenger seat he said regretfully, 'A pity about that. I'd have enjoyed taking you out to dinner tonight, wearing one of your new dresses—the black one.' There was a reminiscent look in his dark grey eyes. 'I can't wait to see you wearing that again.'

But he wouldn't, would he? Jessamy thought to herself as they threaded their way through the traffic towards the open country. Whenever she wore the dresses he would be far away. And a very good thing too, she told herself with a tiny shiver.

The fairytale afternoon faded all too fast into a barely credible memory. Indeed, if Jessamy hadn't had the evidence of the three beautiful gowns hanging in her wardrobe in their dust-bags she might have thought she'd dreamed it all.

When she and Luke got back to the marina they found customers already waiting for the inn to open, and they continued to roll up all evening, in cars, using the new road and parking lot, and on foot. Jessamy had never known the place to be so busy, and with Barry absent, Luke had to take over his duties serving in the second bar.

It was as if all the locals and their regular visitors from farther afield had decided they must make the most of these last few chances to visit the old canalside inn as it always had been, before the transformation took place. The evening developed into one big party, and Friday lunchtime and evening were just the same. By the time Jessamy put the towel up on the beer pumps for the very last time on the Friday night and locked the door behind the last customer, she felt unutterably weary.

And the really hard work hadn't even started yet, as she discovered on Saturday morning when she and Luke began clearing the decks ready for the builders to start work on Monday morning.

First the bars had to be cleared, all the bottles and glasses crated up and carried down to the cellars, which were not going to be affected by the alterations, for storage. And then the furniture, the tables and chairs and rugs from the floor had to be taken down there too, manhandled down the dark, narrow steps and stacked in piles reaching the ceiling. Luke co-opted one of the mechanics to help with all this, but Jessamy had to admit he did the work of two men himself.

Curtains had to be taken down and all the knick-knacks and ornaments, the old horse brasses and traditional canal ware, the water cans and bowls gaily painted in the age-old designs of roses and castles had to be taken from their shelves and niches and packed away, together with the collection of old canal prints that hung on the walls.

By six o'clock that evening Jessamy felt hot, sticky and absolutely filthy, every bone in her body aching with weariness, and they had yet to start on clearing the kitchen which was to be very much enlarged in the improvements.

'I know what you meant now, about earning my extra salary,' she said, ruefully rubbing her back as Luke locked the cellar door securely.

He smiled, dropping his arm carelessly round her

shoulders as they walked together along the passage. 'I couldn't have wished for a better helpmate. You've worked like a Trojan, Jessamy.'

It was a compliment, but she was too much aware of the pressure of his arm on her shoulders to appreciate it.

He laughed down at her, taking in the wisps of hair escaping from her ponytail and the smudges of dirt on her perspiring face. 'And to show my thanks— Cinderella *shall* go to the ball! Or rather, a slap-up dinner. What about the Sun at Sutton Wavell?'

The Sun was an old coaching inn about four miles the other side of Market Swinford and the best restaurant for miles around. Jessamy had never been there, but she'd certainly heard of its reputation for excellent food. The thought of being taken there by Luke brought a spurt of excitement she was immediately ashamed of. 'You really don't need to thank me, and certainly not as extravagantly as that,' she said stiffly. 'Besides, you'll never get a table there on a Saturday night.'

'Care to bet on it?' he challenged with all the arrogance of a man whose wealth could always buy him anything he wanted, even someone else's business. 'So go and take a long, leisurely shower, put on your warpaint and one of your new gowns. Lift-off will be at eight o'clock.' He was taking her acceptance for granted.

But Jessamy knew the popularity of the Sun and the need to make an advance booking, especially at the weekend. When they were full, they were full, and it would take more than the banknotes Luke would undoubtedly flash around to make any difference. The urge to see him fail for once to get what he wanted was irresistible. She didn't think he would be a good loser.

'Thank you,' she said meekly, her lashes veiling the mischievous anticipation in her eyes. 'You're very kind.'

It wasn't exactly a leisurely shower, as the water was cold, but when she had soaped away the stains of the day's labour and let the invigorating needles rain down on her she felt sharply alive. Towelling her freshly washed hair till it was almost dry, she pinned it up on large rollers to give it some bounce and while it finished drying, gave her nails a manicure and completed it with a coat of pearly coral lacquer.

Make-up had never been her strong point as she used it so rarely, but now she took great pains, especially with her eyes, carefully smudging a frosted brown shadow on to her lids and darkening and lengthening her lashes with mascara. A whisk with a blusher brush, a shimmer of lipstick to match her nails and she was ready to brush out her hair and slip on the black dress. When she finally surveyed herself in the full-length mirror she could hardly believe the transformation. The brown eyeshadow made her eyes look even bluer and the blusher emphasised cheekbones she never knew she possessed, and with the bangs of her shining blonde hair swept softly to one side and the back pinned up on the crown to cascade down again in soft waves and curls, she was no longer the fresh-faced ingénue but a woman—even, perhaps, beautiful?

The startling thought had hardly occurred to her when there was a knock on the door of her houseboat. By the time she had reached the saloon Luke had let himself in.

Jessamy stared at him. He was actually wearing a dinner jacket! Black bow tie, ruffled shirt and all. She had never been taken out to dine by a man wearing full fig before. The black, stylishly cut jacket of the formal dress made the dark V of his hairline even more dramatic and contrasting with his slight tan, added such depth to his grey eyes they looked almost black.

It took a moment or two to recollect her reason for accepting his invitation, and when she did she almost hugged herself with delight. With both of them dressed up to the nines it was going to be even more humiliating for him when they were turned away from the restaurant.

He took her hands. 'You *can't* be the same little girl I knocked off her bicycle!'

She wanted to pull her hands away from his touch, but the expression in those deep-set eyes held her immobile, so great was his physical magnetism. She found herself trembling, and wondered if her desire to see him humbled wasn't leading her into deep waters.

During the drive, while the liquid notes of a Mozart piano concerto playing on the car tape deck trickled down her spine, Jessamy kept her mind firmly on Luke Monro's come-uppance. As she had anticipated, the walled yard behind the old coaching inn was packed with cars and he had difficulty finding a parking space. And when they entered by a side door straight into the cocktail bar of the restaurant she was gratified to see how many people would witness Luke's futile attempts to gain a table. Already his commanding self-assurance was attracting attention—especially female attention.

'What would you like to drink?' He was holding her lightly, his hand cupped under her elbow as he steered her towards the bar, and she was very conscious of his dangerous attraction.

'Don't you think you ought to make good your boast about getting a table first?' she suggested. 'You can see for yourself how popular this place is.'

'No hurry,' he said easily, but there was a distinct gleam in his eye. 'Now, what'll it be? Sherry? Martini?'

She compressed her lips at his arrogance and was tempted to refuse a drink but then thought better of it. 'Martini, please. Sweet.' She perched on a bar stool someone else had just vacated.

When the drinks arrived, Luke clinked his glass against hers. 'To a very——' he hesitated as if choosing the right word carefully, '—stimulating evening, Jessamy.'

His eyes held her challengingly until she had to turn away to break the tension. Her glance fell on a portly, greying-haired man standing in the doorway surveying the room. Following her glance, Luke put his glass down and stepped forward, his hand outstretched. 'Cliff! Good to see you again.'

'Luke, you old son-of-a-gun!' The grey-haired man was pumping his hand enthusiastically and beaming from ear to ear. 'How long has it been? Twelve months if it's a day.'

'Jessamy, I'd like you to meet an old friend—Cliff Winters.' Courteously Luke drew her forward to make the introduction and she couldn't help but be aware of the older man's speculative curiosity as she shook hands and murmured a polite greeting.

Luke cast her a sly, sidelong glance. 'Jessamy's worried that you'll be too full tonight to find us a table, Cliff,' he said to his friend.

'And turn you out into the cold unfed?' Cliff Winters chuckled. 'No chance of that, Miss Daunay. I'll come back and tell you when your table's ready. Perhaps you'd like to see the menu while you wait?' He reached a large leather-bound folder from the bar and handed it to her.

She thanked him, opening it out and ducking behind it to hide her chagrin. Cliff Winters must be the owner! No wonder Luke had been so confident. She should have known a man like him would be sure of his ground.

'I can hear you grinding your teeth from here,' he said softly.

Startled, she lowered the menu and looked straight into his mocking eyes. 'Come now, Jessamy. You're not going to be a bad loser, are you? I won the bet fair and square.'

'Only because you had no compunction about trading on friendship, no matter how badly you put that friend out,' she retorted, stung by his taunt.

'Not at all.' The voice was silky but the brows lowered ominously as if she'd touched a nerve. 'Our reservation was made two days ago.'

She stared at him. Two days ago! That must have been after he professed to be disappointed at not being able to take her out after their shopping expedition.

'But you didn't ask me until this evening. You were very sure of yourself, weren't you? Suppose I'd declined your invitation?'

A slow smile curled his lips and made his dark eyes gleam. 'You're here, aren't you?'

A tide of heat suffused her body, staining her bare neck and cheeks, as she realised the predicament her desire to see his arrogance humbled had put her in. She hadn't even considered this possibility, of actually finding herself dining out alone with her employer, a man she despised for his unprincipled business methods, a man she instinctively distrusted, even feared, but who at the same time could exert such a disturbing attraction.

## CHAPTER FIVE

THEY were shown to a small table by a window overlooking a pretty garden, a table made private by heavy red curtains suspended on brass rings dividing it from the tables either side. And in the centre of the starched white cloth was a single long-stemmed red rose in a silver holder, its petals just beginning to unfurl.

'Cliff always was a romantic at heart.' Luke lightly

stroked the edge of a petal with his thumb, smiling as if he approved of this touch.

To cover her confusion, Jessamy leaned forward and buried her nose in the rose's centre, but drew back disappointed. 'It doesn't have any scent!'

'Nothing in this life's *quite* perfect. Or——' Luke let his eyes travel slowly over her, eyes that were appreciative yet held a gleam of mockery, 'or very little.'

The waiter arrived just then with their first course and the wine waiter to display the bottle for Luke's approval, taking his attention away from her. The food was excellent, but Jessamy found it hard to relax in such insidiously romantic surroundings; the rose on the table, the red wine in the crystal glasses glowing like rubies in the light from the pink-shaded lamps, and a piano playing soft, nostalgic tunes from a distant corner. Even the moon hung yellow beyond the leaded panes of the window, though the sky was still not quite dark.

Aware of her own susceptibility to the forceful man sitting across the small table, she tried to appear unruffled. 'This is just the kind of place I'd like to own one day,' she commented.

Luke's eyebrows soared. 'I thought the height of your ambition was to run the kitchens in *my* restaurant! Is that why you took up cooking—with a view to becoming a restaurateur one day?'

'Why not?' she said sharply, suspecting he was laughing at her. 'Or are you one of these men who can't bear to think a woman might be as good at running a business as he is?'

'I don't think—I *know*,' he taunted. 'Don't most women learn to cook in order to catch a husband? You know—the way to a man's heart——'

'No, they don't!' Jessamy's slender body was rigid with indignation, her blue eyes sparking. 'Of all the complacent, chauvinistic attitudes! You wouldn't accuse me of angling for a husband if I'd trained as a—as an accountant, so why should being trained as a professional cook be any different? It happens to be something I love doing and know I do well, so why shouldn't I aim to make a career of it?'

Luke leaned back in his chair, watching her with every indication of enjoyment. 'What makes you so sure you *are* good? Even half as good as the chef here?'

'What makes you think I'm not?' she flung back at him. 'Don't tell me! Because I'm a woman, and no woman could ever do anything as well as a man.'

'Well, for all your vaunted ambition, you haven't shown much evidence of your genius yet,' he said silkily. 'If you're as well qualified and talented as you claim, why did you find it so hard to get a job?'

'You have the nerve to ask me that!' Jessamy pushed her half-eaten *gazpacho* away feeling another mouthful would choke her. 'In case you hadn't noticed, we're in the middle of a recession, and unfortunately employers are all men like you these days. They don't only ask for first-class qualifications but they demand experience too, though how I was expected to get that experience——' She turned her head away to gaze unseeingly out of the window, blinking back tears of angry frustration.

'It's a cold, hard world.' There was some sympathy in Luke's voice, but Jessamy was too incensed to notice. 'Just as a matter of interest, how did you come to hear of the job Barry had on offer? He surely didn't advertise it in the national press.'

'No, I wrote to him, among several hundred others.' As she told him about it, some of the desperation she'd felt at that time washed over her. 'I was working my way through the catering section of the Yellow Pages county by county. Most of my letters went unanswered, of course. A few wrote a polite note declining my services, but only Barry offered me a job.'

There was an odd expression in his dark eyes. She would almost have taken it for admiration if it hadn't been for the quirk of his mouth. 'So being a girl of ambition and resource, you saw yourself turning Barry's little one-horse pub into a mecca for gourmets?'

Did he have to be so hatefully mocking? It hadn't been at all like that. Months of constant rejection had all but annihilated her confidence and she had been humbly grateful to Barry for offering her work—any kind of work. Not that she meant to admit it.

'That's right.' Her chin came up defiantly. 'Barry had great plans for the marina until——'

'Until you discovered he was all talk and no action,' he broke in, and before she could retaliate he swept on, 'But didn't your family object to you working at the marina?'

She was surprised into an involuntary, 'Why on earth should they?'

He paused while they were served with their *tournedos en croûte* and a dish of vegetables that was a work of art and almost too pretty to disturb. 'Don't be deliberately naïve, Jessamy. You shot me down in flames for daring to read anything into the set-up I found at the marina, but surely your father must have seen the dangers of the situation, a young girl living on the premises with her boss without a chaperone.'

'You sound positively archaic,' she scoffed. 'And anyway, my father died years ago.'

'Your mother, then,' he pressed, and for the life of her Jessamy couldn't stop the revealing flush staining her cheeks. 'You mean you've never told her what the set-up was?'

'What was the point when she couldn't do anything about it?' she said defensively.

His eyes narrowed. 'Why couldn't she?'

He was like a dog worrying a bone. 'Because she lives on the other side of the world,' she said unwillingly.

'She went out to Australia to make her home with my married brother just before I left college.'

'She left you to fend for yourself!' Luke looked so shocked she leapt to her mother's defence.

'Why not? I'm a big girl now, and Steve needed her. Avril—my sister-in-law—had a bad car accident and Steve had no one to cope with the children. Anyway, Mum needs to be needed, and I was always too independent for her to cosset.'

'You weren't tempted to go with her?' He topped up her wine glass.

'I still had my final exams to take,' she reminded him. 'And everything was arranged in a rush after Avril's accident. Mind you,' her eyes clouded, 'if I'd known the months I was going to spend looking for work I might not have been so sanguine about sending her off with my blessing. It wasn't much fun, living in a grotty rented room on unemployment benefit.'

'I don't imagine it was,' Luke said grimly. 'So why didn't you follow her later? With a home to go to and your qualifications, you might have found it easier to find work in Australia.'

'And how was I supposed to find the fare when it took me all my time to pay my rent?' she retorted. Really, he had no idea how the other half lived!

'Surely your family could have helped, knowing how you were placed?' The betraying flush stained her cheeks again and he stared at her disbelievingly. 'You didn't tell them you couldn't find a job, did you?'

'Don't you think they'd got enough on their plates with Avril in a wheelchair and suffering from suicidal depression without having them worry about me?'

'I didn't realise it was as bad as that. I'm sorry.'

'Well, it was. It still is. A few white lies didn't seem such a crime if it preserved Mum's peace of mind.'

'Quixotic, but hardly a crime,' Luke agreed, his dark eyes resting on her with a peculiar softness so that she toyed nervously with the food on her plate. 'You must miss your family very much, Jessamy.'

'Of course I miss them.' When one of the long, newsy letters came she missed them unbearably. 'But——' she smiled philosophically, never realising the heart-catching wistfulness her eyes revealed, 'Australia's hardly a place you can pop over to for the weekend.'

He took her hand, the gentle caress of his thumb sending electric tingles through her skin. 'You'll visit them one day.'

'It's a lovely thought.' She sighed. 'But I can't see it happening in the foreseeable future.'

'It might be sooner than you think,' he said lightly.

'Oh yes, when I've made such a success of running your new restaurant I can retire early with my loot,' she retorted, laughing, realising how the atmosphere between them had changed, as if in drawing out her confidences he had also drawn off some of her antagonism.

He released her hand. 'I've never said you'll get the job. I might have something very different in mind for you,' he added cryptically.

Her curiosity was aroused, but he refused to be drawn and she had to drop the subject when the waiter came to take away their plates and another to wheel up the dessert trolley. 'I can recommend the profiteroles,' Luke suggested. 'They melt in the mouth.'

But Jessamy was eyeing the fresh fruit. 'You wouldn't deprive me of my first strawberries of the season, would you? If I take your suggestion I might not be able to get into this beautiful dress again. No wonder your friend Cliff is so well rounded if he eats his own gorgeous food!'

'I'll take the risk of becoming well rounded like him,' Luke grinned. His grin widened as Jessamy concentrated her attention on the succulent strawberries, letting each one burst in a small explosion of sharp sweetness on her tongue. 'Thank heavens for a girl who enjoys her food,' he added.

Jessamy giggled. 'Am I making a pig of myself? I'm afraid I always do over strawberries. They're my weakness.'

'Not at all,' he said politely. 'You've no idea how disheartening it is for a man if his companion picks at her meal as if it's an insult to expect her to eat it.'

'And you——' she tipped her head coquettishly, '—have had vast experience of taking ladies with the appetites of birds out to dine.'

'Fishing, Jessamy?' That sardonic left eyebrow rose again, but his eyes were still smiling. 'All right, while I don't claim my experience is *vast*, I have wined and dined quite a few ladies in my time, though never one as appreciative as you.'

'I expect it's with me being in the business. Food, I mean. I know the effort that goes into each dish, so I could never insult the chef by sending it back picked over.' His lips twitched at her seriousness.

'I've got something to show you,' he said when they'd finished their coffee. Taking her hand, he led her out through the french windows.

The mossy flagstones led down in three shallow-stepped terraces into the shadows. Jessamy took a deep breath of the sweet-scented air and exclaimed in delight, 'Oh, it's a herb garden!'

'I thought it would appeal to you.' They had moved away from the light spilling from the restaurant windows, but the moon had found a break in the surrounding trees and its pale luminescence emphasised Luke's dramatic good looks, highlighting his strong cheekbones and adding a silvery sheen to his dark hair while leaving the expression in his eyes hidden in deep, mysterious pools. Very gently his hands cradled her slender neck and chin.

She knew what was coming. Part of her, the sane,

down-to-earth Jessamy warned her to cut and run, but sanity was suspended under his spell. As his mouth found hers, her own responded, her bones melting at the warm, searching pressure. It was the sound of footsteps on the flagstones that brought her back to earth, and as the restaurant owner blurted, 'Oh, I do beg your pardon!' she shivered.

Luke released her without haste. 'That's all right, Cliff, we were coming in now anyway. Jessamy's getting cold.'

'As long as I'm not interrupting,' said Cliff, and in spite of the shiver, Jessamy felt anything but cold. She burned with embarrassment.

'Things have quietened down now,' Cliff went on. 'And I couldn't let you leave without offering you my congratulations, Luke. I hear you've at last got your hands on that marina you were after. So how long is it going to be before you start trying to put me out of business?'

Jessamy hardly heard Luke's answer. Embarrassment at being caught in Luke's arms was nothing compared to the wave of self-loathing that washed over her now at this reminder of the true nature of the man she had been responding to with such abandon moments ago. How could she have been so naïve as to fall under the spell of his practised charm? How could she have forgotten for a moment what he was really like? How he must be laughing at her now behind that enigmatic mask of his! This whole seductive evening had been planned deliberately to disarm her, and she'd fallen for it.

Well, never again, she swore to herself as, their goodbyes said, she walked stiffly beside him back to the car. 'I'm sorry about that. Cliff may be a romantic, but he has no sense of timing,' he said with a grin as he handed her in.

'On the contrary, I thought his timing was perfect,'

she flashed back at him as he slid into the seat at her side.

'Temper, temper!' Luke's grin was broader still. 'Is today's hard labour catching up on you?' He switched on the tape deck and drew smoothly away.

Jessamy closed her eyes, but far from relaxing, she seethed while the strains of the *Eine Kleine Nachtmusik* only increased her contempt for him. Didn't he ever give up? Or was his conceit so great he couldn't conceive that she had seen through his shallow charm? She had begun the evening with an urgent desire to see his arrogance humbled, and now the desire was even more intense. It was that very arrogance, his certainty that she must find him irresistibly attractive, that put the weapon into her hands.

It was bright moonlight when they got back to the marina and Jessamy stalked angrily ahead as they crossed the parking lot. Catching up with her, Luke took her arm. 'Watch your step. We can't have you ending a perfect evening taking a header into the canal!' And because the shadows hid the treacherous unevenness of the path, she had to bear with his touch that seemed to burn her through her thin wrap.

'And the evening's not over yet,' he said softly as they reached her houseboat. 'Not quite.' He pulled her expertly into his arms, drawing her softness to him, welding their bodies from lips to thighs until she could be in no doubt of his desire for her. She had to fight her own desire leaping at once to meet his, a battle she came near to losing as his kiss went on and on until she felt she was drowning.

With a low groan Luke at last lifted his head. 'Jessamy, you witch! What is it about you? How do you make me feel like this?'

'Like what?' She felt breathless and dizzy from his onslaught on her senses and from the desperate necessity to keep her head.

He gave a low laugh, dropping his encircling arms to the base of her spine and pressing her to him. 'Like I can't wait to get you into bed.'

Jessamy gasped. She wouldn't have believed it even of *his* overweening conceit! 'So this is where I'm expected to pay for my evening's entertainment, is it?' she flung at him in white-hot anger. 'Well, let me tell you something. You may not be able to wait to get into *my* bed, but I can happily wait till doomsday to get into *yours*! I don't share your alleycat morals, and I find your charm very easily resistible!' She pushed against his chest with a force that took him by surprise, and stumbling on the uneven path, he crashed backwards into the bushes. Not stopping to see if she had damaged more than his self-esteem, Jessamy locked the houseboat door behind her.

It was odd that now she had achieved her ambition of denting Luke's arrogance she found little pleasure in it. Not that she regretted her violent reaction to his suggestion of how they should finish their evening. It was true she didn't share his lack of morals, not quite so true that she found him easily resistible. But she was uncertain what his reaction would be to his set down, and she couldn't help but remember there were still two days to get through alone with him at the marina before Barry returned, and another week after that before she would be able to put a safe distance between them when she took up her new duties.

So it was with some trepidation that she crossed to the inn on the Sunday morning to begin clearing out her kitchen ready for the builders. She was packing the contents of her cupboards into crates when Luke walked in, and so tense and nervous was she, the basin she was holding dropped through her fingers to shatter on the tiled floor.

'I'm glad that wasn't aimed at my head,' he said

dryly. 'I can see your temper hasn't improved since last night.'

'There's nothing wrong with my temper!' she snapped, angrily fetching a dustpan to sweep up the broken pieces.

There was a long scratch down Luke's cheek and he ran his fingers over it gingerly. 'I can only hope I'm not around when you're really riled!'

'You asked for it,' Jessamy muttered.

'Well, I'm damned if I'm going to apologise for what I said.' His voice had a hard, unyielding note. 'Any red-blooded man would fancy taking you to bed. But I did *not* intend to exact payment for taking you out.'

'Then you shouldn't have made it sound as if you did,' she retorted hotly. 'You can hardly blame me for pointing out—rather forcibly, I will admit—that when you got your hands on the marina it didn't entitle you to get your hands on me!'

'I never thought for one moment it did,' he said wearily. 'Really, Jessamy, I find your attitude juvenile and hysterical.'

'Because I don't fancy you making love to me?' she jeered. 'Yes, I can understand what a blow that must be to your pride.'

'I think my pride can stand it. And anyway——' his flinty eyes raked her from head to toe, 'I'm rapidly cooling off the idea.'

'Hooray for that!' she muttered under her breath, picking up a heavy box of crockery and struggling to the cellar with it. And he let her.

They toiled through the day, Jessamy tight-lipped and silent with hostility, Luke equally silent and managing to ignore her most of the time, pausing only briefly for a snack lunch which they each took on their own houseboat, and too exhausted by evening to do anything but fall into bed.

Bang on eight o'clock the next morning the builder's

lorries rumbled up. Luke was already waiting for them and in no time at all the plans were laid out, a brick-end weighting down each corner against the breeze, while the ground was measured out for the foundations.

Curiosity prompted Jessamy to wander over to watch and she was amazed to see the area the new buildings were to cover; amazed and resentful when she saw how the original old waterside inn was going to be dwarfed by this ambitious new extension. Barry's plans had been much more modest, much more in keeping. History obviously had no place in Luke Monro's book. It wouldn't bother him that he was ruining the character of the place as long as he got the profits rolling in. She wanted to protest, but his engrossed face as he leaned over the plans with the foreman warned her it would be futile.

But when she saw him pointing up to the ruined lock-keeper's cottage at the top of the flight of locks and overheard him say, 'The demolition people start up there next week and will be bringing the stuff down by barge,' she could keep her tongue between her teeth no longer. 'You're not pulling it down!' she burst out. 'Surely not even *you* could be such a vandal! That's been a landmark around here for generations.'

Everyone had stopped what they were doing to stare. Luke turned round slowly, his black brows glowering. 'Yes, I'm pulling down the old ruin—if it's any business of yours,' he said in a voice that would have warned her he was holding on to his temper with great difficulty.

'It's the business of anyone who knows this place,' she flung at him, and rushed on bitterly, 'Isn't it enough that you're destroying the whole character of the inn with your grandiose schemes?'

In one stride he had grasped her arm with a grip that dug agonisingly into her flesh and was dragging her willy-nilly along the path and into the inn, slamming open the door of his office with the flat of his hand and hurling her inside so that she fetched up painfully against the desk.

'I will *not* have my actions questioned in front of the workmen,' he ground out, closing the door and advancing on her threateningly.

'You won't have your actions questioned—period!' She rubbed her sore arm and bruised hip, fighting to hold back her tears. 'You hurt me, you bully!'

'Not nearly as much as I'd like to hurt you.' The menace in his voice made her quail, but there was nowhere to retreat to with the solid desk at her back. She had no alternative but to face his rage. 'There's no reason why I *should* explain myself to you, but if it's the only way of stilling your viper's tongue . . . I'm pulling down the cottage because it was a condition laid down by the local council. The place is a danger to the public. And as for my destroying the character of the inn—on the contrary, I'm spending a great deal of money to ensure the new buildings *will* be in character. The keeper's cottage isn't just going to be flattened. It's going to be taken apart piece by piece and the sound materials incorporated in the buildings here.'

Jessamy's face burned while her stomach lurched emptily. It seemed that once again she had allowed her antipathy to provoke her into hurling accusations at him without being sure of her facts. And once again she'd made an utter fool of herself. But just because he'd been able to justify his actions it didn't mean she resented him any the less. 'I might have known you'd have an answer,' she said bitterly. 'And I only have your word for it that the council are insisting the cottage must go.'

'And my word is obviously not good enough for you.' His narrowed eyes were iron-hard and his mouth curled contemptuously. 'Just what is it you have against me, Jessamy? It can't be that I was unwise enough to admit I'd like to make love to you. You were hostile before that.'

'You really need to ask?' she choked, and plunged on wildly, 'The country must be strewn with people who have cause to resent you, if you make a habit of cheating people out of their livelihood as you did Barry!'

'Cheating?' he said softly, but with a menace that made her go cold.

'All right, maybe it wasn't strictly illegal,' she conceded angrily. 'But you certainly can't say it was straight or honest.'

He stood staring down at her for several seconds longer, his mouth compressed, then he turned on his heel to the door. 'Don't make judgments on something you know nothing at all about,' he snapped coldly.

'I notice you don't try to justify yourself this time,' she flung after him. 'Because you can't!'

Luke snatched open the door. 'I've justified myself enough for one day. It's a waste of breath anyway, trying to change your bigoted opinion.'

Jessamy stood there for a long time after Luke had walked out, struggling against the feeling that somehow she had come off badly in that exchange. She was still shaking when she finally quitted the office to go back to her houseboat, just in time to see Lambury's delivery van unloading all their goods on to the car park.

'Can't you carry it in for me?' she protested, hurrying across.

'Got a lot on the van today. Besides, you don't look short of helpers.' The van driver jerked his head towards the gang of building workers.

Jessamy didn't dare take the men away from their job and not for anything would she ask Luke for help. Manfully she struggled along the towpath with box after unwieldy box, stacking them in the saloon of her boat.

She was still ticking each item off against the delivery note when Luke stuck his head round the door. 'I have to go into Market Swinford to see the architect. If you want something to do you can stitch these on to the new bedlinen.' He tossed a package at her.

She let it fall, fiercely resenting the implication that she'd been slacking. 'Aren't you afraid they'll dig a hole in the wrong place if you're not there to watch them?' she jibed.

His eyes glittered. 'Not much fear of that, as it's their lunch break.' Moments later she heard his car roar away.

It was all right for those who could treat themselves to business lunches, she thought waspishly, bending to pick up the package and finding a bundle of woven name tapes bearing the marina's new insignia. She finished checking the goods and after a hasty snack, began the tedious job of stitching the tapes on to every pillow-slip, duvet cover and towel.

It was five o'clock in the afternoon and Jessamy was just finishing her mammoth task before Luke appeared at her door again. 'You're not still at it!' He frowned and sounded angry.

She flushed with resentment at the sharp reproof. 'I'm sorry if I don't work fast enough to come up to your exacting standards, but I was trained to cook, not sew.'

He sighed heavily. 'I didn't mean that at all. For pity's sake leave it now. I didn't say the job had to be finished today.'

Jessamy stretched to ease her cramped limbs, or rather, she tried to, but every way she moved she came up against a pile of boxes. 'Just how am I supposed to cope with all this stuff stored in here?' she said crossly.

'You won't have to. Barry should be back at any moment and we can shift stuff on to *Hyacinth*,' he reminded her. 'I thought he'd be here by now.'

Now it was Barry who was falling short of their boss's expectations, she thought sourly. She couldn't help a feeling of relief at the prospect of his return. Barry would at least provide a buffer between her and Luke, and surely by now he would have recovered from the mild insanity of thinking he wanted to marry her. She glanced out of the window up the flight of locks, willing the hotel-boats to appear. 'I'll take a walk up to the top to see if he's in sight yet,' she said. 'I could do with some fresh air and he'll need help with the lock gates anyway.'

To her surprise Luke followed her when, instead of making back to the marina and crossing the canal by the bridge near the inn, she set off up the towpath and round the far end of the lagoon, scrambling surefootedly up the steep bank that brought them on to the canal by the third lock gate.

'Can we get across here?' Luke queried doubtfully.

'Of course.' Jessamy stepped lightly across the narrow footbridge with a handrail only on one side. 'It's quite safe.'

Luke followed more cautiously, halfway across pausing to look down at the dark, greenish water far below at the bottom of the steep, narrow walls. 'I wouldn't want to use this bridge in the dark!' He stepped over quickly to Jessamy's side.

She was uncomfortably aware of the tension and constraint between them as together they moved steadily up the rising towpath, the only sounds the crunch of their feet on the gravelled path and the twittering of the birds in the hedgerow.

'Once the holiday season gets under way, this stretch will be alive with cruisers and pleasure boats making their way up and down,' she commented to break the unnerving silence.

Luke looked back down the flight of locks to the marina at the bottom and then up at the still distant top. 'What happens when a boat starts down from the top at the same time as another one starts up from the bottom? They wouldn't see each other till they met halfway.'

'On a short flight they'd make sure their way was clear before they started,' she explained. 'But on a long flight like this there's a passing pond halfway. Look, there's ours.' She pointed across the canal to a reed-bordered pool. 'The first one to reach it slips in there to wait for the other boat—or boats—to pass.'

They walked on several paces in silence and then he said with a curious note in his voicee 'You really love this place, don't you?'

'Who wouldn't? I mean, just look at it.' She swept an arm round to encompass the rolling green fields undulating to meet the blue sky, the woods and coppices and the mellow red brick village nestling against a far hill where the sun caught the gilded weathercock on the sturdy church spire.

'And you wouldn't ever want to leave it?' he probed.

Jessamy wondered what he was getting at. Her eyes flew to his face, but she could read no clue there. Was he trying to tell her that after their latest row he was having second thoughts about keeping her on here?

'I wouldn't *want* to,' she said, her backbone stiffening, because she'd be damned if she'd take a word back. 'But I know we can't always have what we want in this world. At least, most of us can't.' She hadn't been able to resist that last dig, but when Luke made no further comment she couldn't help feeling uneasy.

At the top of the flight of locks she paused to look sadly at the old keeper's cottage, trying to imagine what the spot would look like when it had been obliterated. It didn't look in such a dangerous condition to her.

'Still sentimentalising over the old ruin?' There was a hard edge to his voice. Almost, she thought, as if some of her accusations had got through his thick skin.

'Oh, I realise you have no room for sentiment,' she retorted, 'But it isn't only sentiment that makes me believe it's a mistake to pull the place down. In summer a lot of boats have to wait up here to use the locks, a captive clientele if this place was done up as a shop and cafeteria.'

Luke looked thoughtful, scanning the sweep of canal where it broadened out from the topmost lock gate, and then turning back to look at the cottage. 'You could be right,' he said surprisingly. 'Oh, not about trying to restore the cottage. It's too far gone for that, and anyway I need the materials for the extension to the inn. But I must admit your point about offering a service to boats up here makes sense. Maybe we could put a new building up on the site. And before you start blistering my ears with your opinion of ugly modern concrete blockhouses,' he added with a challenge, 'I visualise something rustic that'll blend in with the countryside.'

Jessamy flushed because those caustic words *had* been hovering on her tongue. 'I suppose something like that might be all right,' she conceded grudgingly.

'Shh! Can you hear something?' Luke had his head on one side, listening.

Jessamy listened too and caught the sound of a distant chug-chugging. 'It's coming!'

All differences forgotten in the excitement of the moment, Luke grabbed her hand and as they started running along the towpath, the nose of the leading boat appeared round the bend. They stopped at the splendid sight as the narrow boats drew nearer, the sun gleaming on the brand new paintwork. Barry raised his hand to wave as he caught sight of her, beaming all over his sunburned face, but Jessamy hardly noticed him.

'They're decorated, Luke!' she cried out in delight, feasting her eyes on the riot of colour as she saw that the doors opening on to the well deck and all the side panels between the windows were painted in the traditional designs of green and red and gold, pictures of wildly improbable castles and rioting roses. 'Oh, how beautiful!' Forgetting all constraint in an excess of excitement, she threw her arms around his waist and hugged him.

'I'm glad I'm able to do *something* right!' he said, his hands lying lightly on her shoulders and one eyebrow lifting sardonically.

Her hands dropped to her sides in embarrassment as she realised how she'd let herself get carried away. Tensely she turned from Luke's mocking gaze to watch the boats drawing into the side, just in time to see Barry's beaming smile turn into a scowl.

'Pass me the windlass, Barry,' she called, hoping he wouldn't notice her burning cheeks, but he was still scowling as he leaned out until she could reach it.

'Can I help?' Luke followed her to the first lock and would have followed her too as she skipped lightly over the narrow footbridge, but she waved him back. 'All right, but stay that side and when I say push, lean against the balance beam to open the gate.'

She fitted the windlass to the spindle of the top lock, gripping the metal bar firmly as she wound the paddles up to open the sluice below water level. After she had removed the windlass she called, 'Now, Luke!' and together they pushed the two balance beams projecting across the towpath each side of the canal until the gates swung open.

Barry manoeuvred the boat into the lock and Jessamy went into reverse, swinging the beams the opposite way to close the gates, then carefully winding down the paddles again. Then they moved on to the next set of gates where she wound the paddles up to let the water out of the first lock and into the second. When the two levels had evened, they pushed on the balance beams again to allow Barry to move the boat one step down.

Closing and opening, they worked their way down the long flight, and it was getting late by the time both boats were safely moored at the marina. Jessamy was hot and very tired but she still couldn't resist jumping aboard *Tiger Lily* to inspect what would be her domain for the coming weeks.

The driving deck at the rear opened straight into the galley and she ran her fingers admiringly over the neat, shining fittings, opening cupboards, peeping into the oven and the large fridge, deciding where all her new utensils would go, then passed on into the dining area where the two tables, each seating four people, were spaced wide enough apart to make serving the guests easy, and then on into the stateroom, which seemed enormously roomy yet cosy, fully carpeted and curtained with a heater against one wall, a small bar tucked into a corner and plenty of comfortable chairs.

Coming out on to the well deck at the front of the boat, she sprang ashore and would have begun to explore *Hyacinth* which held all the sleeping accommodation if Barry hadn't protested, 'Hey, what about some food, Jess? I haven't eaten since midday. Don't say you've got nothing ready for me!'

She felt a stab of guilt because she *had* forgotten, but at the same time she wondered how she was supposed to prepare a meal *and* labour to open the lock gates. 'You must be starving. Come on over to my boat and I'll rustle something up,' she said.

She was annoyed to find herself feeling nervous as she moved some of the boxes to make a place at her table for him. 'I'm sorry about the lack of space,' she apologised. 'I shan't take long. Will a fry-up be all right?'

She would have hurried into the galley, but he caught her hand and held her back. 'That can wait for a minute. Come and say hello, Jess.'

'I already have,' she protested, eyeing him apprehensively.

'Not properly.' He tried to pull her into his arms, but she held back.

'Barry—please! Don't start all that again.'

His face reddened. 'Start what?' he said bitterly. 'I can't even touch you without you jumping like a startled rabbit. You weren't so choosey with Monro. I saw you, throwing yourself at him.'

She turned away to hide her burning cheeks. 'That was only because I was excited, seeing the boats.'

'And don't you think *I* was excited, seeing you again?' He pulled her round to face him. 'Jess, I've had six days puttering along that canal with only Dave to talk to and little to think about but you—us.'

'Oh, Barry . . .' She heaved a despairing sigh. 'I hoped you'd have forgotten all that nonsense.'

'Nonsense! I'm crazy about you and you write it off as nonsense?' He glared at her in baffled anger.

'I'm sorry.' She hated to see him upset and not be able to do anything about it.

'Then you *have* been thinking about it while I've been away?' he said eagerly, mistaking her apology for a change of heart. 'I've thought of nothing else.'

Jessamy knew if she thought about it till she was ninety she wouldn't feel any different, but she wanted to let him down as lightly as possible. 'Of course I've thought about it, and that's why I'm convinced it would be a mistake. Barry, can't you see? We just wouldn't be right for each other.'

'No, I can't,' he insisted stubbornly. 'Jess, we've always got on well together, so why have you suddenly turned against me?'

'I haven't!' She ran her fingers through her hair in exasperation. 'I feel exactly the same about you as I always have—as a good friend. I'm sorry, Barry, but I can't see you as anything more.'

His stocky shoulders slumped and Jessamy hoped that at last he was coming to his senses and was ready to accept there could be no future for them as anything but friends. It was a false hope.

'It's Luke Monro, isn't it?' he accused. '*He's* the big boss around here now, so he's obviously a better prospect than me. Even if I hadn't actually seen you throwing yourself at him I'd have known there was something going on between you. You're as jumpy as a pea on a drum whenever he's around.'

'Now you're being ridiculous! If I'm jumpy with him it's because we had a couple of flaming rows while you were away.' But she couldn't stop the fiery flush creeping up her cheeks as she remembered her uninhibited response to Luke's kisses.

Barry stared at her for long moments. 'I don't believe you,' he said at last, and made for the door.

'Where are you going? Barry, what about your meal?'

'Suddenly I'm not hungry.' He slammed the door behind him.

For the next few days Jessamy did her best to avoid both men as much as possible as she worked hard preparing the boats for their first trip, making up the beds with their pretty duvet covers and matching pillow-slips, laying out the matching towels and a bar of scented soap in each cabin, stocking the bar in the stateroom and choosing a selection of books and magazines for the use of the guests, checking her menus, baking things that would keep, getting in enough dry goods to stock her galley and making a list of fresh meat, fish, fruit and vegetables to be delivered on the morning of the day they sailed.

She cooked the meals for herself and the two men in the hotel-boat galley to accustom herself to the new stove, but it wasn't an ideal arrangement. There was still a tangible tension between herself and Luke however naturally she tried to behave, and Barry mostly sat silent and glowering at the table, his eyes flicking from her to Luke as if watching for proof of his suspicions that there was something going on between them.

Preoccupied as Luke was with overseeing the building work, she thought he hadn't noticed Barry's boorish behaviour, but she should have known nothing ever got past his sharp eyes. It was after lunch on the day before they expected their guests to arrive when he asked with apparent idle curiosity, 'What's biting Barry these days?'

Jessamy was glad to have her head bent over the washing up. 'Why don't you ask him?' she hedged.

'I already have. He was uncommunicative to say the least, though I got the definite feeling I'm *not* his flavour of the month! I thought you might know what's bugging him. He's hardly going to make a successful host for the next couple of weeks in this mood.'

Jessamy was relieved that Barry hadn't openly accused Luke. That would have been too embarrassing. But she didn't see why Luke shouldn't be made to realise he was to blame. 'It's what becomes of trying to manipulate other people's lives,' she said with some asperity. 'It was *you* who put the idea of Barry marrying me into his head and now I can't shift it, no matter how often I say no.' She left it at that. No way could she admit that Barry's disappointment was aggravated by the suspicion that Luke was succeeding with her where he had failed.

Luke was silent for several minutes. 'I'm sorry,' he said at last. 'My jumping to that particular conclusion is causing you a lot of trouble.'

'You can say that again!' she retorted with feeling.

'Well, we can only hope he'll eventually get the message.' He picked up a clipboard. 'Now I think you and I ought to sort out which guest we're putting in which cabin.'

He helped her on to the bank, along the towpath and on to the butty boat moored behind. 'The married couple, Amy and Brad Francis, had better have the largest twin berth aft,' he said. 'I *had* thought of giving Miss Mortimer the other twin up for'ard, but she'll probably complain that it's too far from the showers, so I reckon you'd better have that. You'll be working flat out this trip and you'll need that extra space to relax in. Miss Mortimer can have this single next door to the shower.'

They moved on down the boat, Luke opening the doors of the next three cabins, all singles. 'There's nothing to choose between them, so we'll put Mrs Asher in the first and Desmond Britton next to her.'

'Desmond Britton? Not the man who writes about food and restaurants in the newspapers?' She stared at him aghast.

'The same.' There was a malicious gleam in his eyes. 'Having sudden doubts about the standard of your cuisine, Jessamy? Just remember he can do this operation a lot of good if he likes what he finds—and a lot of harm if he doesn't.'

So she was still very much on probation!

'I've deliberately chosen a very mixed bag for this trip,' Luke went on. 'When we're taking bookings from the general public there's no way we can vet them to make sure they'll get on with each other cooped up on a boat, so you and Barry will have to get used to handling all types and all situations to keep things running smoothly and everybody happy.'

'Yes, I can quite see that,' Jessamy said seriously. She was still a bit subdued as she thought of having her culinary skills judged by such an authority as Desmond Britton, but she tried to put that coming ordeal out of her mind. At least once they set off tomorrow she would no longer have Luke's disturbing presence to contend with. She would be able to bend her mind exclusively to the the job in hand.

'So this last cabin will be empty,' she said. 'Don't you think it might be better if I settled for that instead of the twin?'

'Who said it's going to be empty?' Luke dropped his arm across her shoulders and looked down at her as if he was enjoying some secret joke. 'This will be my cabin. Right next to yours.'

Jessamy's heart seemed to miss a beat and then pick up only to beat twice as fast. 'Your cabin? But you're not coming on this trip.'

'Aren't I? Funny, but I was under the impression I was.' She suspected that under his blandly innocent expression he knew exactly the turmoil of dismay and apprehension his announcement had thrown her emotions into.

'But—but what about the builders?' she said weakly. 'Who's going to supervise the work here and make sure nothing goes wrong?'

'Who else but the architect who drew up the plans and knows exactly what I want? That's why I employed a local man, so he can be on the spot when I can't. Oh no, my dear Jessamy, I wouldn't miss this maiden trip for anything in the world. I look on this as a challenge, a golden opportunity to see if, during the next two weeks of enforced proximity, I can't change the disrespectfully low opinion you have of me.'

And quite deliberately he bent towards her, kissing her very thoroughly indeed.

## CHAPTER SIX

SATURDAY dawned grey and dull, but by early afternoon the clouds were rolling away before a brisk breeze and the sun began to shine. Jessamy had woken early and had transferred the clothes and personal belongings she would need for the next two weeks—including of course the three new evening dresses—from her houseboat to her cabin aboard the floating hotel before breakfast. She had taken delivery of the perishable foods and packed them away in the refrigerator, done some of the preliminaries for the meal she intended to serve that evening and made sure the first aid box had everything they could possibly need for minor injuries and complaints. Luke had attended to the filling of the freshwater tanks and checked that they had a couple of spare gas cylinders for the stove, and one of the mechanics refuelled the boat while Barry did a last-minute check over the engine.

By early afternoon Jessamy had changed out of her jeans and sweater into a crisp shirtwaister with matching sandals and was trying to find small tasks to occupy herself as she nervously waited for the first guests to arrive.

'No need to look as if you're facing execution!' Luke laughed, giving her shoulders an encouraging squeeze. 'You might even enjoy it!' And from the wicked gleam in his eye she knew he wasn't referring just to her work.

Barry who, as she had feared, felt his suspicions confirmed by Luke's apparent last minute decision to come with them, made a disgusted 'Pshaw!' and took himself off to tinker with the engine again, leaving Luke to step forward with her to meet the first arrival as a red, open-topped sports car roared up the road towards them. Even at a distance, Jessamy could see the driver's long dark hair streaming in the wind. The car screeched to a halt only feet away.

'Darling Luke, how *did* you find this hideaway? I got lost *three* times in spite of your instructions. Still, I'm here now, all ready to make whoopee!' The girl swung agilely out of the car and flinging her arms around Luke, kissed him soundly.

She was the most beautiful girl Jessamy had ever seen, dark enough to have Latin blood in her veins, hair black as a raven's wing and naturally curly, large, dark chocolate eyes fringed with long, sooty lashes. She had the perfect bone structure that would preserve her looks into old age and her skin was lightly tanned and flawless. A head taller than Jessamy and voluptuously built with curves in all the right places, shown off by a mint green outfit she wore with careless elegance, the slacks hugging her hips and thighs so closely Jessamy couldn't help wondering how she got them on and off, and the matching shirt unbuttoned far too low for decency.

'Hello, Bianca,' Luke greeted her with the easy familiarity of someone who knew her very well indeed. 'I must say you look stunning as usual, though I'm afraid you're going to be a bit short on males to wow this trip, unless you fancy trying your skills on Desmond.'

The girl's full lips made a fetching moue. 'Not my style, darling. But I'll have *you*, won't I?' She pulled Luke's head down to those inviting lips again, and he was anything but unwilling.

At last Luke seemed to remember Jessamy's presence. 'Bianca darling, come and meet your hostess, Jessamy Daunay. Jessamy, this is Miss Mortimer.'

'I'm pleased to meet you, Miss Mortimer,' Jessamy said politely, lying in her teeth, because for some unaccountable reason she had taken an instant dislike to the girl.

The dark eyes raked Jessamy from head to foot and her handshake was little more than a brief touch of her long, elegant fingers. 'Hello.' She sounded bored and turned immediately back to Luke. 'Well, darling, where's this fabulous marina you've been waxing so lyrical about?'

Luke spread out his arms. 'This is it.'

Bianca's face was incredulous. 'This! But it's no more than a rundown hovel!'

Jessamy drew an indignant breath and waited for Luke to put this superior little madam in her place. But he only laughed. 'Well, I have to admit it doesn't look much yet. But wait till I've finished with it.'

'But, darling . . .' Bianca fixed her large eyes on him reproachfully, 'you can't mean to bury yourself in this awful place for ever!'

'For as long as it takes,' Luke laughed. 'Now let's get your luggage and I'll show you your cabin.'

Bianca flung open the boot of the little red car and Jessamy saw it was crammed with matching suitcases. Enough clothes, she thought sourly, for a world cruise. Even Luke looked dismayed. 'Can you give me a hand with the smaller cases, Jessamy?' he asked, and festooned with baggage he led the way with Jessamy struggling in the rear while between them Bianca stepped lightly, free and unfettered.

'Oh, isn't it dinky!' she squealed when they got below, but as Luke opened her cabin door her face dropped. 'I didn't imagine it was going to be as small as *this*, darling. Where am I going to put everything?'

'I was wondering that myself.' Luke heaved the two largest cases on to the bed. 'I think you've over-provided for this kind of trip. You won't need half this stuff. Suppose we leave one of your bags behind here?'

She stared at Luke as if he'd gone off his head. 'Darling, don't be ridiculous! How do I know what I'll need till the time comes? You'll have to find room for it all somewhere.'

Jessamy was only too happy to leave the two arguing when she heard another car approaching. This time it was an unpretentious black saloon, and as she saw the lone man emerge she guessed this must be the famous writer on food and critic of restaurants. Nervously she greeted him. 'Mr Britton? I'm Jessamy Daunay, your hostess. Welcome aboard.'

He was a man in his late forties, tall and very thin, wearing impeccable white canvas shoes, white drill slacks and a thick fisherman knit sweater, his thin, overlong grey hair lifting from his balding head in the light wind.

'Miss Daunay.' He shook hands, but his eyes went past her to the gleaming boats and a slight shudder shook his stringy form. 'A bit garish, aren't they? But then I suppose all these bright colours are supposed to be traditional.' He had a precise, rather high-pitched voice which struck Jessamy as old-maidish, and her heart sank. This was the man who could make or break the hotel-boat enterprise by what he wrote about it, and instinctively she knew he was going to be very hard to please.

'If you'd like to come this way, sir, I'll show you to your cabin.' She noted with relief he had only brought one suitcase. But it was a large one and Jessamy doubted she could manage it herself, so she called to Barry to ask if he would help. Barry, still making adjustments to the engine, straightened up and wiped his oily hands on a rag.

'Not with those filthy hands, he won't!' Desmond Britton said shrilly and picked up the bag himself. And as he followed Jessamy on to the boat she knew there was already a black mark against them.

Well, Luke had only himself to blame, she thought angrily. If he'd been there to help instead of dancing attendance on Bianca Mortimer . . .

Fortunately Desmond Britton made no comment on the smallness of his cabin and merely nodded when Jessamy suggested he might like to go along to *Tiger Lily* to meet the other guests when he had unpacked.

Almost immediately a third car arrived, and this time it was the married couple, Amy and Brad Francis. Amy Francis was about thirty, Jessamy judged, painfully thin in a girlish Indian muslin sundress that exposed her white, bony shoulders and stick-like arms, so thin that seeing her mop of improbably red hair Jessamy was put in mind of a long-handled feather duster. Her husband was some years older, once a very handsome man but paunchy now, with thickening jowls and thinning hair. He held Jessamy's hand just a little too long when she introduced herself, and she was quickly aware of the hostility this roused in his wife's hazel eyes.

Well, Luke *had* said it would be a mixed bunch this trip, she thought gloomily as she escorted them below, moving quickly to evade Brad's attempts to pat and touch her when he thought his wife wasn't looking. And they were certainly mixed so far—a spoiled beauty, a finnicky bachelor and now a man with a wandering eye and even more wandering hands and his possessively jealous wife. Heaven only knew what the final member of the party would be like.

This time Barry had cleaned the engine oil from his hands and helped with the baggage without being asked, and as they left this latest set of guests to unpack neither he nor Jessamy could help hearing Bianca Mortimer's excited laughter or help seeing right into her cabin through the wide open door. It was a chaotic scene, bags half unpacked with garments strewn everywhere and Bianca wafting a diaphanous black nightie before Luke's face.

Jessamy, averting her eyes and feeling unaccountably sickened, hurried past, but Barry caught up with her, his fingers biting into her arm. 'And you thought he'd decided to come on this trip for your sake!' he jeered. 'You don't think Luke Monro's going to look at *you* now?'

Jessamy drew away from his touch. 'As any interest

Luke had in me was purely a figment of your imagination,' she snapped, 'I don't see that it matters a rap that he's brought his girl-friend along.'

Of course it didn't matter, she reiterated to herself as she made her way back to *Tiger Lily*. If Luke Monro fancied the spoilt Miss Mortimer they were two of a kind and deserved each other. But for some reason her voice was unusually sharp when she got back to the galley to prepare tea for the guests and found Desmond Britton there, poking his long nose into her store cupboards and wiping his hand over the working surfaces as if expecting to find dust or grease. 'I don't think you need fear food poisoning,' she snapped. 'It's perfectly clean.'

'Yes, I can see that.' He seemed unperturbed by her tartness, but his narrow face didn't relax a fraction as he went on, 'I must say I'm quite impressed. You don't have much space, but it's very workmanlike.'

Jessamy found herself softening towards him. 'Would you like some tea, Mr Britton? I was just going to make some.'

'Thank you, Miss Daunay. That would be very acceptable.' he said formally. 'I suppose it's too much to hope for Lapsang Souchong?'

'Certainly, sir.' Jessamy enjoyed her small victory in being able to accede to his request as the dried-up little man's face, while not actually breaking into a smile, brightened visibly. 'If you'd like to relax in the stateroom I'll bring you a tray.'

Amy and Brad Francis were the next to join them, Amy's only stipulation being that her tea should be served with lemon, and Brad ogling her with heavy gallantry and declaring it would taste like nectar when served by such a pretty waitress. Jessamy was pleased to notice Desmond Britton had already demolished two of her chocolate éclairs and Brad Francis took one eagerly, but Amy gave the delicacies a horrified look and shook her head. 'Very appetising I'm sure, but *so* fattening!'

Jessamy was beginning to wonder when Luke was going to tear himself from Bianca's arms and come and welcome the rest of his guests when they both arrived, Bianca greeting Desmond Britton almost as exuberantly as she had first greeted Luke, much to that gentleman's discomfort, and then moving on to Brad Francis who wasn't at all averse to her charms, and finally laying a cool cheek against the equally cool cheek of Amy Francis. Jessamy asked if she would like some tea.

'Not if you've only got that awful stuff Desmond's drinking.' Bianca wrinkled her nose. 'It smells like creosote!'

'Perhaps Earl Grey would be more to your taste, Miss Mortimer,' Jessamy suggested, keeping her temper with difficulty.

'It'll do, I suppose,' the girl said indifferently.

To Jessamy's discomfiture, Luke followed her back to the galley. 'Sorry I wasn't more help. Bianca does expect rather a lot of attention.'

'I didn't expect you to help,' Jessamy said coolly, lying in her teeth again. 'I mean, *you're* not a member of the crew, are you?'

He was standing a little too close for comfort and the gleam in his eye wasn't all amusement, more as if he'd like to put her over his knee and spank her, but before he could say a word, Bianca cooed, 'Darling, what *are* you doing in the kitchen?'

For just a fleeting second Jessamy could have sworn a flicker of annoyance crossed Luke's face, but she must have been mistaken for the next moment he was smiling indulgently down at the beautiful, pouting face turned up to his.

'Not kitchen, Bianca. On board it's known as the galley.'

Bianca smiled seraphically, but there was malice in

the dark eyes that flicked a glance at Jessamy. 'That must make you the galley slave, then.'

'Jessamy's here to look after you and to do her best to make your trip happy, but she's nobody's slave,' Luke said crisply. 'Though if you're really interested I'm sure she'll be happy to show you round her galley.'

'Me? Darling, you know I can't even boil water.' As Bianca retreated back to the stateroom with Luke in tow he grinned back at Jessamy as if to say, 'There, I knew *that* would get her out from under your feet!'

'When are we going to get moving?' Bianca was saying impatiently as Jessamy placed her tray on a low table in front of her. 'Or are we going to spend the whole two weeks gazing out over a builder's yard?'

'Just as soon as the last guest arrives,' Luke soothed. 'Mrs Asher's coming by train, but I arranged for a taxi to collect her at the station.'

'This looks like it now,' said Jessamy, going to the open door on to the well deck.

'Asher—Asher—I don't think I know any Ashers,' Bianca mused aloud. 'And I thought I knew all your friends, Luke.'

'You *have* met her, quite a few times, though I doubt if you'll remember.' Without turning round Jessamy knew he was smiling.

'I've never met that!' Bianca said, scandalised, as the spritely figure got out of the cab and demanded of the driver in a strident cockney accent, ' 'Ow much, then, ducks?'

Hastily Jessamy clambered on to the bank to meet the newcomer, and even she had to admit the elderly little woman cut a quaint figure. A pair of surprisingly shapely legs teetered in very high-heeled white shoes, but the body above was shaped like a dumpling that strained the seams of a purple satin dress to bursting point. White hair frizzed till it looked like a dandelion clock bobbed above a round, very red and perspiring face, and a white fur cape, the cause of her discomfort, was clutched round her shoulders.

'Mrs Asher—let me help you with your bags,' said Jessamy when she'd introduced herself. There was only one suitcase, a battered affair with a broken clasp held together by a leather strap but there were innumerable carrier bags.

'Call me Minnie, ducks, everybody does. Cripes! 'Ave I gotta climb in there?' She teetered up the gangplank and gave a raucous squeal as the boat rocked slightly under her weight. 'Cor, I need me 'ead inspectin', comin' on a lark like this,' she giggled breathlessly, then her eyes widened as Jessamy opened the cabin door and ushered her in.

'Ooh, ain't it lovely! I never seen anythin' like this before!' She bounced on the bed, then sprang up to open the wardrobe. 'An' even a washbasin all me own!' She tried one of the taps and squealed when hot water gushed out.

Jessamy couldn't help but be touched and warmed by her pleasure in everything. 'Would you like to unpack first, or would you rather come along to *Tiger Lily* straight away for a cup of tea?' she asked.

Minnie Asher fanned herself with her hand. 'Oh, me bits an' pieces can wait if there's a cuppa goin'. Me tongue's hangin' out.'

'Perhaps you'd like to leave your cape?' Jessamy suggested, but the little woman clutched it to her fiercely.

'Not on yer life! If I've got to meet all them posh folks I've gotta keep me end up. It might've seen better days, but it's still a good bit o' fur. It was give me by one of the ladies I cleans for——' She clapped her hand over her mouth. 'Oh, lor! Now I've gone an' let the cat out of the bag. Mr Luke says I wasn't to mention I was 'is char.'

Jessamy could hardly keep her face straight at

Minnie's consternation, but at the same time she was surprised that among all his fine friends invited on this trip, Luke should have included his cleaning lady. All right, remembering his remark about having to help people of widely different tastes and backgrounds to mix happily together on the cruises she realised he had an ulterior motive, but even so the generous gesture didn't seem in character.

'It's all right, Minnie. I won't give your secret away,' she smiled. 'It makes no difference to me anyway. You're a guest and it's my job to see you enjoy yourself. So let's see about that tea, shall we?'

'Thanks, ducks.' Minnie looked relieved. 'Not that *I* mind any of 'em knowing, but Mr Luke thought maybe I shouldn't let on.' So Minnie was still perspiring under her fur cape as Jessamy helped her off *Hyacinth* on to the towpath.

'I see that Bianca's one of the party.' Minnie jerked her head towards the red sports car. '*She'd* be in if she fell in. Don't know what Mr Luke sees in 'er—toffee-nosed little madam. Why 'e can't find 'isself a nice girl like you to settle down with I don't know. No sense at all, men.'

Jessamy hastily explained that all the daytime facilities were aboard *Tiger Lily,* hoping Minnie's voice was not carrying as she feared it was.

As soon as she had introduced the little lady to the rest of the party and had settled her comfortably in the stateroom with her tea tray they were off, Jessamy and Luke together working the long flight of locks. When the last gate was finally negotiated they were able to climb aboard and relax, or rather Luke was able to relax, claimed immediately by Bianca. Jessamy had all the tea things to wash, but even she found it restful to watch the rolling countryside slowly unfolding through the window as she worked.

She wasn't left in solitude for long. After a few

minutes Minnie Asher teetered into the galley. ' 'Ere, give us a cloth and I'll wipe for you, ducks.'

'But Minnie, you're supposed to be on holiday,' Jessamy protested.

The older woman shifted her shoulders uncomfortably beneath the white fur cape. 'All them empty fields—it ain't what I'm used to. 'Ouses an' streets—that's more my line. I'd take it kindly if you'd let me give you an 'and now and again.'

'But of course you can if that's what you'd like,' Jessamy said at once, though she felt sad that Minnie couldn't appreciate the lovely countryside.

Minnie grabbed a tea-towel, brightening visibly. 'I never seen *anythin'* like these boats before—and this kitchen!' Her eyes darted everywhere as she worked.

'I think Luke hopes to have a whole fleet of these eventually, if this one's a success,' Jessamy told her.

'So 'e was sayin' just now.' Minnie's eyes sparkled gleefully and her voice dropped to a hoarse whisper. 'That Bianca wanted Mr Luke to put 'is money into a gambling casino, but 'e wasn't 'aving any. You'd 'ave thought that'd show 'im what she is, but no.' She shook her head gloomily. 'She means to 'ave 'im, you know.'

That much had been obvious to Jessamy ever since the little red car had roared up to the marina, but to have it confirmed by Minnie gave her a strangely hollow feeling inside. 'Perhaps she *will* make the right kind of wife for Luke,' she said.

Minnie made a rude noise. 'If there's one thing you can say for Mr Luke, 'e ain't stuck up. but *'er*! Not one word 'as she said to me yet, nor even looked in my direction. That Amy Francis did just pass the time o' day an' that 'usband of 'ers, 'e's all right. Even that dried up old stick Mr Britton tried to be polite, but not 'er. Oh no, far beneath 'er ladyship's notice I am.'

'Minnie!' Luke's voice came sharply from the doorway. 'What on earth are you doing in here?

Nobody expects you to work your passage. This is supposed to be a rest for you, so go and put your feet up and make the most of it.'

Looking sheepish, Minnie dropped the tea-towel and scuttled out.

When the door had swung to behind her Luke said tightly, 'I'd be grateful if you didn't encourage her to gossip, Jessamy.'

Red-faced, Jessamy wondered how anyone could be expected to stop the little cockney woman talking, but he went on, 'And I'd rather you didn't take advantage of her good nature.'

Her temper sparked. 'I had no intention of taking advantage of her,' she snapped. 'But I was under the impression it was *my* job to keep the guests happy, whatever they wanted to do. And Minnie made it obvious she was happiest lending a hand. At least *I* talk to her, which is more than the other guests appear to do!'

A faint flush appeared under Luke's tan. 'That's nonsense. Of course they're talking to her.'

'Are they? Do they really care that she's utterly out of her element here, not only with the company but because she's not used to so much empty countryside? Are they really trying to make her feel welcome?'

Luke looked furious at her tirade, but before he had the chance to retaliate the door swung open again and Bianca said peevishly, 'Luke, it's all very well for you to come and hide in here, but you inflicted that awful woman on us, so the least you can do is protect us from her. For pity's sake come and see if *you* can stop her talking!'

Jessamy shot him a triumphant glance as he followed Bianca back to the stateroom. But being proved right did nothing to abate her anger. How dared he accuse her of encouraging Minnie to gossip? And as for telling her not to take advantage of a guest's good nature . . .

Did he think the generous gesture of bringing Minnie along on the trip was enough? Didn't he care if the poor woman was miserable for the two weeks?

They moored for the night about six o'clock, drawing close in to a grassy bank that gave a good foothold for getting from one boat to the other. They had passed several boats going in the other direction, but now the empty canal curved away out of sight behind a wood and the only sign of human habitation was the tip of a church spire peeping over a distant hill.

Jessamy began the serious business of cooking the dinner while Barry cleaned up to take on his duties as barman. Most of the passengers strolled as far as the wood to stretch their legs before going back to *Hyacinth* to change for the evening.

It was important that this first meal should be as near perfect as she could make it. If she could please Desmond Britton at her first attempt he might be prepared to overlook any slight slip in standard should the right kind of supplies ever be difficult to come by.

She had decided to start with avocados stuffed with prawns, going easy on the garlic in the dressing until she learned the guests' tastes, followed by pork spare ribs in barbecue sauce accompanied by honey-glazed new potatoes and mixed vegetables *en papillote*. The apricot cheesecake she had made the day before had only to be decorated with cream.

By the time everything was ready the guests were drifting back to the stateroom where Barry revived them with drinks. Leaving the meal in the heated cabinet, Jessamy slipped over to the other boat to shower and change. She had already caught a glimpse of Bianca in a stunning flame-red dress that plunged to her navel in front and even farther at the back, and Jessamy had actually slipped on the kingfisher blue silk, one of the three dresses Luke had provided, when she abruptly changed her mind.

She wasn't here to compete with Bianca, she reminded herself, and it would be no contest if she tried. Angry with herself, she put on one of her own dresses, a simple peasant style that left her shoulders bare.

Whether it was her own sharp words to Luke that had borne fruit or whether Minnie Asher had worked her own brand of charm on the other guests Jessamy didn't know, but she was quick to notice as she served the dinner that Minnie was looking happier and much more at ease. Brad Francis delighted in her outspoken comments and egged her on while Minnie preened under his heavy-handed gallantries. Amy Francis seemed a lot less uptight, probably becuse the elderly little cockney lady who was claiming her husband's attention was no threat to her, and even Desmond Britton laughed at some of Minnie's sallies. Only Bianca studiously ignored her still, and having penned Luke into the corner seat, was addressing her low-toned conversation solely to him as if they were alone at the table.

'Does that dressing have any cream in it?' Amy Francis demanded when the avocado was put in front of her, and when Jessamy admitted it did, she scraped all the prawn filling out and made only a couple of dips with her spoon into the plain avocado before pushing it away. It was the same with the barbecue sauce on the spare ribs. Every scrap was scraped off before she attempted to eat, and then she only picked at it. 'I have to watch my figure,' she whispered to Jessamy with a strained smile.

Such waste of good food, particularly when she had laboured over it herself, usually annoyed Jessamy, but she could only feel sorry for Amy. She was painfully thin and would have looked more attractive with a little more flesh on her bones, but Jessamy guessed Brad Francis' wandering eye had something to do with Amy's obsession about putting on weight, as if the poor woman believed that only by strict dieting could she keep him.

'I must say you've got a lovely way with veg,' said Minnie, smacking her lips appreciatively when Jessamy cleared the plates. 'I don't know as I've ever 'ad 'em so tasty.'

'I'll second that,' Desmond Britton chimed in, and Jessamy flushed with gratification. *'En papillote?'* he questioned, and she nodded.

Minnie demanded, 'What's that in plain English?'

Jessamy explained that each serving had been wrapped in an individual foil parcel with butter, herbs and a little stock. 'It saves fuel as the parcels can be cooked in the oven with the main dish and it means none of the flavour and goodness is lost,' she finished.

Bianca sighed heavily. 'I didn't bargain on a cookery lecture with my meals.'

'I'm sorry.' Jessamy whisked the plate from in front of her, resisting the urge to tip the leavings over her arrogant head. She hurried back with the apricot cheesecake, which Amy Francis refused with a shudder and only nibbled a few cherries and grapes from the bowl of fruit Jessamy had also provided.

When she had served coffee and petits fours in the stateroom, Jessamy could at last relax and eat her own meal. Barry had already had his out on the rear deck in the sunshine, and was now ready to resume his duties as barman, so she was able to enjoy a few minutes' soothing solitude. Not that it was all that soothing when she could still hear Bianca's voice cooing in the stateroom.

After she had cleared up in the galley Jessamy went through to the stateroom herself to see if anyone wanted anything, but Amy and Brad, Desmond and Bianca were absorbed in a rather acrimonious game of bridge while Luke talked to Minnie.

'Is it all right if I go out for a breath of fresh air?' she asked him quietly. 'I'll be back to make some more coffee later.'

'Yes, quite all right. You don't need to ask.' He was still stiff with her and although she had not mentioned Bianca by name, she knew Luke hadn't forgotten her implied criticism of his girl-friend.

The sun was a great red ball slipping away behind the wood. It was so quiet she could hear the tall grasses rustling as she walked through them and the yellow pollen from the buttercups dusted her sandals. She slipped them off, wriggling her toes in the cool grass, and then, confident of her complete privacy, she began to dance towards the wood, leaping high in the air and twirling round, happy to be in such a lovely spot and even happier to have these few minutes of freedom away from everyone's beck and call. Just as she reached the fringe of the wood she dropped down, breathless.

She didn't hear the swishing of the long grass until Luke was standing over her. 'I saw this wood nymph dancing,' he smiled, 'and then she disappeared on a puff of breeze.'

'Oh!' Jessamy scrambled to her feet in confusion. 'Does someone want me?'

He put a calming hand on her arm. 'No, I told you, your time's your own now. But Minnie was convinced you'd either get lost or the werewolves would make off with you if I let you go alone.'

She couldn't help the bubble of laughter that rose up in her. Minnie Asher no more believed in werewolves than she did herself. This must be the little cockney's way of scoring off Bianca, sending her boy-friend after another girl. 'Oh, Minnie——' She shook her head, laughing still. 'She's a great character. I'm glad to see her settling down happily after all.'

'Yes, I must apologise for Bianca's behaviour, not only towards Minnie but to you too,' he said quietly. 'She's not usually such a little snob.'

Jessamy's eyes widened. It couldn't have been easy for a man like Luke to feel obliged to apologise for the girl he loved. Her eyes widened still further when he went on, 'Look, there's a path through the wood just over that stile. Put your sandals on and let's see where it leads.'

He held her hand to steady her over the stile and seemed to have forgotten to let it go again as they wandered into the wood, but Jessamy was so conscious of it she was tongue-tied. He only released her hand when he spotted a branch of a tree overhanging the path and with a whoop like a schoolboy he leapt up, caught hold of it and swung up and down several times before dropping on to his feet again.

Infected by his burst of exuberance, Jessamy boasted, 'I bet I can do that.' She sprang up, catching hold of the branch all right. But her weight wasn't sufficient to make it swing, and suspended like that she had no way of knowing how far away the ground was.

Luke doubled up with laughter until she wailed, 'I'm stuck! Oh, Luke——' Her hands lost their grip and she plummeted down to bounce against Luke's broad chest, sending them both sprawling. But instead of helping her up, his arms imprisoned her, his lips claiming hers as if they belonged to him.

Her struggles were only token as the sensuousness of his kiss sent ripples of delight through her nerves. She wound her arms around his neck, twining her fingers in his thick dark hair as she responded.

'Jessamy—Jessamy——' he breathed against her hair, and the heat of his breath was enough to trigger off new sensual responses. His hands stole inside the wide neck of her peasant style dress, caressing the smooth skin of her back, and when they slipped round to cup her breasts, squeezing gently, teasing the thrusting nipples, she thought she would die of the melting, urgent sensations. Her whole being yearned for this devastating man, demanding her surrender.

And then clearly on the still evening air came the sound of Bianca's plaintive call. 'Luke—Luke, where are you?'

He raised his head. 'Hellfire and damnation!' Then he smiled at her conspiratorially. 'She'll never find us here.'

He would have kissed her again, but for Jessamy, Bianca's voice had brought reality. Cold horrible reality.

What was Luke up to? Wasn't Bianca, beautiful as she was, enough for him? It was by his invitation that she was accompanying him on this trip and it was obvious to everyone there was a very close relationship between them. So what was he doing, giving her the slip and skulking in the woods, making love to someone else?

The answer was crystal clear. Because that someone else—herself—had shown herself to be eager and available. She burned with shame at the abandoned way she had behaved, and sobbing, she tore herself out of his arms and stumbled back along the darkening path.

Bianca was halfway across the field and moving towards the wood. 'Where's Luke?' she demanded as Jessamy ran past her.

'He—he's coming,' she choked, but didn't stop.

As she stumbled towards the boats she heard Bianca demand angrily, 'Luke, what the hell have you been doing? That girl had *grass* in her hair!'

Luke's reply was drowned by a sudden ominous rumble of thunder and by the rattle of her heels on *Hyacinth*'s gangway as she rushed to her cabin.

# CHAPTER SEVEN

THE thunderstorm that had raged long into the night made it even more difficult for Jessamy to sleep, and she was glad when it was time to get up to prepare the early morning tea for the guests. The storm had broken the good spell of weather and rain dripped dismally down the windows, echoing her low mood. She slipped on a waterproof anorak to run the short distance to *Tiger Lily* and the galley, and she knew she was in for an uncomfortable time carrying the tea trays back to *Hyacinth* on a morning like this.

She managed it in two trips, taking the bull by the horns and knocking on Bianca's door first. The girl stirred languorously at the brisk, 'Good morning. Your tea, Miss Mortimer.' But Jessamy could feel the resentful dark eyes on her back as she put the tray down and beat a hasty retreat.

That Bianca had every reason for her resentment, Jessamy was only too well aware, but the attitude of the other passengers puzzled her. When she took in the Francis' tray Brad said with a leering smile, 'Ah, the naughty Jessamy,' and Amy almost snatched the tray from her, bundling her out of the cabin as if she might contaminate them.

On her second trip Minnie Asher heaved herself to a sitting position and said gleefully, 'You certainly gave that stuck-up little madam something to think about last night!' Before she could ask the questions that were obviously hovering on her tongue, Jessamy excused herself.

Even Desmond Britton made the dry comment, 'So haute cuisine isn't your only talent, Miss Daunay.'

But Jessamy was too preoccupied with that last tray to make anything of the strange comments. She had left Luke's tray till last because she was reluctant to face him again, especially in the privacy of his own cabin. But it had to be done, and squaring her shoulders she rapped on his door.

He called, 'Come in,' and she found him already dressed in black slacks and a thin black sweater that clung to his muscular chest, sitting on his bed with a detailed map of the canal system spread out beside him. As she crossed the cabin to put his tray on the bedside table he stood up and shut the door, leaning against it. 'You certainly let me in for a rollicking last night,' he said grimly. 'Whatever possessed you to run off like that? If we'd just strolled back together——'

'You'd have been able to pretend to Bianca we were only out for an innocent walk?' she broke in.

'Something like that.' His face was unreadable as he looked at her and Jessamy was aware of the figure she must cut, the bottoms of her jeans sodden from several journeys between the boats through the wet grass and the front of her hair dripping where it had escaped from the hood of her anorak.

'I'm afraid I'm not very well versed in the kind of games you play,' she retorted.

'Games?' he said softly.

'Well, what else would you call it when you invite your girl-friend along and then try to make love to *me*?' she choked.

'Jealous, Jessamy?' There was a light in his eyes that made her heart beat faster, but she was determined that this time she wasn't going to let him get through her defences.

'Jealous? Don't flatter yourself,' she flung at him.

He moved as swiftly as a black panther, taking her so completely by surprise she had no chance to guard against the leaping response to his deep, searching kiss.

He raised his head and there was the light of victory in his eyes. 'Oh, but I think you are.'

'You—you must be the most conceited, detestable man I've ever met!' she gasped, tears springing to her eyes. She pushed with all her force against his chest, this time taking *him* by surprise, and snatching open the door, almost cannoned into Bianca wearing a glamorous satin negligee, her hand still upraised to knock.

There was just time to hear the other girl's sharply indrawn breath and her furious, 'You again!' before she fled.

There wasn't even time to pull herself together, because when she reached the galley to start preparing the breakfasts she found Barry there. 'You certainly made a fool of yourself last night,' he said sourly.

She took off her wet anorak and surreptitiously wiped her face on the sleeve of her sweater, glad of the rain that disguised her tears. 'I don't know what you mean,' she said stiffly. It was the first time she'd been alone with Barry since they'd left the marina and she was very wary of him.

'Enticing Luke Munro off to the woods with you, that's what. *And* letting Bianca catch you at it,' he added.

'I did not "entice" him!' Jessamy denied hotly.

Barry was openly disbelieving. 'When everyone saw you whispering to him, and a few minutes later he was following you out? Try convincing Bianca it wasn't deliberate! The things she called you when she was tearing a strip off Luke! We all heard her, every word.'

Jessamy's cheeks burned like fire. So *that* was the reason for all those cryptic remarks from the guests when she had taken them their tea! They all thought she was deliberately setting her cap at Luke, trying to entice him away from Bianca! 'It wasn't like that . . .' she said wretchedly.

'No? Why else won't you look at me, then, if you're not besotted with him and determined to land him?' His face was set and his eyes resentful.

For just a moment Jessamy wondered if it wouldn't solve all her problems if she announced her engagement to Barry. It would stop Luke playing cat and mouse games with her and it would give the lie to Bianca's ugly accusations.

But that would be using him, and though his persistence irritated and upset her he deserved better than that, because she knew she would never go through with the marriage.

'For the umpteenth time, Barry,' she said, trying to keep her temper. 'I don't love you, and it would make no difference if Luke Monro had never been born.' She saw he was still prepared to argue, so she slapped the frying pan down on the top of the stove. 'Now please let me get on. They'll be here for their breakfast in a minute.'

'Why is it I've been given the smallest and noisiest cabin on the boat?' Bianca asked loudly when the whole company were seated at the table and Jessamy was serving cereals and fresh grapefruit.

'I thought that one would be the most convenient for you as it's next to the shower,' said Luke, pouring her coffee. 'And anyway, all the single cabins are the same size.'

'It's like Piccadilly Circus,' she retorted, pouting. 'People in and out all the time and the water rushing and gurgling.'

'I'm sure you're exaggerating.' Luke put the coffee pot down with a bump.

'No, I'm not!' She darted a venomous glance at Jessamy. 'I notice *she* gave herself a double cabin. If anyone's going to have all that space and comfort it ought to be one of the guests, not the staff.'

'*I* allocated that double cabin to Jessamy,' said Luke with a distinct edge to his voice. 'She works very hard and deserves room to relax when she's off duty.'

Jessamy was uncomfortably aware that all eyes were on her, Bianca's furious and the rest openly speculative at hearing Luke take her part. 'If Miss Mortimer wishes to change cabins with me I'm perfectly willing,' she said with quiet dignity.

Now Luke looked furious. 'There'll be no talk of changing. It'll take too long and cause far too much upheaval.' There was a note of finality in his voice that Bianca must have recognised, for she pushed her chair back in a temper and stormed out.

Luke didn't move a muscle, he merely said, 'Get on with serving the breakfast, Jessamy. Miss Mortimer has apparently lost her appetite.'

Jessamy sighed and went back to the galley to fetch bacon, eggs and sausage and the fluffy little potato cakes she had made. They hadn't been on this cruise twenty-four hours yet and there were still thirteen more days to go, she thought with dismay.

When everyone but Amy, who was still picking like a bird at her unsweetened grapefruit, had been served, she replenished the coffee pots and refilled the toast racks and took the croissants out of the oven where they had been heating.

'Can we get moving yet?' Barry asked impatiently when she returned to the galley.

'Just give me five minutes to collect the early morning tea things and make the beds,' she begged, whisking past him.

She knew her own cabin didn't need attention as she'd tidied it before she'd left, so she started with Luke's and worked down the boat, leaving Bianca's cabin till last in case that was where the girl had taken herself off to sulk. But when she finally tapped on

Bianca's door there was no reply. Pushing the door open, she stopped on the threshold in horrified amazement.

The cabin was chaotic, but it was all Jessamy's own clothes and belongings that were heaped on the bed and scattered on the floor, not Bianca's.

'Hurrying back down the boat, she flung open the door of the double cabin that she had been occupying. Bianca turned from the wardrobe where she was hanging up the last of her dresses. 'Well, you did say you were willing to change with me,' she said sweetly.

Jessamy bit back the hot protest that she hadn't been willing for Bianca to take the law into her own hands, invade Jessamy's privacy and treat her belongings as if they were rags. 'We'll be leaving in a few minutes,' she said coldly. 'So unless you intended to spend the whole morning here gloating, you'd better get back to *Tiger Lily*.' She shut the door with a sharp snap and went back to the other cabin to restore it to something like order.

'You said five minutes,' Barry grumbled when she finally struggled back to *Tiger Lily* herself laden with trays and dirty crockery. He took some of the burden from her and helped her into the stern of the boat. 'You've been at least a quarter of an hour and they're champing at the bit to get moving.'

'I'm sorry,' she said wearily, 'but Bianca decided she wanted my cabin.'

'And you let her!' Luke stepped through the narrow door from the galley. 'I thought I said there was to be no changing, or does what *I* say carry no weight any more?'

Jessamy felt as if she'd done a day's work already that morning and to have Luke hauling her over the coals for something that wasn't her fault was the last straw. 'Obviously not with Bianca,' she flashed at him. 'Why else did you think she stormed off from the breakfast table? And it's no good glaring at me like that. She didn't ask *my* permission to throw all my clothes in a heap into the single cabin.'

His eyes grew cold as stones and his mouth tightened. 'She did that? Moved your clothes out and hers in? Then she can just go and move them all back again!'

He was turning away to find Bianca when Jessamy caught his arm. She hadn't intended to tell tales but he'd needled her. 'Luke—please. Leave things as they are now. I couldn't stand a running battle over it for the next two weeks.'

He stood looking down at her, his mouth still hard. 'I don't like to see her getting away with such high-handed behaviour.'

'But you won't make an issue of it?' she begged.

'Oh, all right,' he agreed reluctantly, but the look in his eyes told her he hadn't relished seeing this side of Bianca's nature.

The boats moved off and Jessamy got busy with the washing up and baking a batch of cakes for tea, and so saw little of the passing countryside. At eleven o'clock she took trays of coffee and biscuits in for the guests. It had stopped raining, but the day was grey and uninviting and they were all in the stateroom with the door to the well deck closed. Desmond Britton was scribbling in a notebook while Minnie entertained Brad Francis with what sounded like a rather ribald anecdote and Luke, Bianca and Amy were playing a three-handed game of Scrabble.

Bianca, Jessamy was quick to notice, looked as happy as a lark now she had got her own way and had found there were no repercussions, and Luke was laughing at something she'd said as if he had completely forgotten his annoyance with her.

The boat cruised on until they reached a waterside pub in time for lunch. It was obviously a popular spot with other canal users, for there were several boats there, and Bianca moaned about having to walk through the wet grass because they had to moor some way away. After being cooped up all morning, everyone was glad of the change of scene and trooped en masse from the boat. All but Jessamy, of course, who had the lunch to cook.

Luke, who was following the others, poked his head round the galley door. 'Can't you spare a few minutes for a quick one, Jessamy?'

She added a deft squiggle of cream to a strawberry shortcake. 'Not if your guests expect a meal ready for them when they get back,' she said briskly. Actually she wasn't *so* pushed for time. The stuffed loin of pork was already in the oven and there was only the sauce to make, a job that could be done while the vegetables were cooking later. But she didn't want to have to sit there and watch Bianca working her fascination on Luke, and neither did she want to cause any more speculation among the guests.

Underlining the thought came Bianca's impatient, 'Oh, do come on, Luke!'

'Can't I at least bring you something across?' he asked, still hesitating. 'A glass of white wine, perhaps?'

'I don't drink,' Jessamy said stiffly, and then flushed as Luke's eyebrows arched and she knew he was thinking of the wine she had consumed that night he'd taken her to dinner at the Sun. And how long ago that seemed now! 'At least, not when I'm working,' she amended.

He shrugged as if to say, well, I tried my best, and a few moments later she saw him leap off the boat into Bianca's waiting arms.

She had been telling herself she was looking forward to this hour or so of peace and quiet on the empty boat, but in reality it wasn't so pleasant, not when everyone else was out enjoying themselves. She felt left out, poor little Cinders left to mind the kitchen. She was ashamed of feeling so sorry for herself, but she didn't seem able to help it. So she was quite glad when Barry returned unexpectedly.

'There's a water tap just down there,' he said. 'I think the hose'll reach, so I'll get the water tanks refilled.'

By the time he had finished Jessamy was also through with the tasks that needed her immediate attention.

'Come on, we've earned ourselves a drink.' He went down the boat to the bar, coming back with a beer for himself and a lager and lime for Jessamy. She joined him on the bench seat beside the tiller and for a time they sat in companionable silence.

'You know, Jess,' he said suddenly, 'I don't think I'm cut out for this lark. Oh, I don't mind driving the boat so much, though it's pretty tame up and down the same stretch of canal. But all this flunkeying—Yes sir, no sir, three bags full, sir. And how would you like your Martini, madam, shaken or stirred?'

It was the first time he had talked to her naturally since he'd got that silly bee in his bonnet about marrying her, and she was relieved. 'Yes, but crewing this boat isn't going to be permanent, Barry, at least not for you. Once the marina's open again you'll be looking after that.'

'I suppose so. But is that going to be much better? I mean, a posh place like Luke intends it to be—I'll still have to play the flunkey, and there'll be all that paper work.' He stared down at his broad, capable mechanic's hands. 'There's not going to be much for these to do. Not much chance of getting to grips with a boat's engine again.'

'Oh, come on, Barry.' She tried to stir him out of his gloomy mood. 'It won't be as bad as that. There'll be free time when you can work on your own boat, and anyway, you'll still be supervising the boatyard.'

He grinned at her. 'Little Miss Sunshine, always looking on the bright side!'

She didn't feel very sunshiny, she thought ruefully,

but was determined not to start feeling sorry for herself again. And it was a relief to have Barry behaving like his old self again. 'Look, when am I going to be able to pick up some more stores?' she asked.

Barry unfolded a map of their route and they were still poring over it, their heads together and their drinks on the bench beside them, when Luke suddenly appeared. 'I thought you'd got too much to do to take a break, and that you didn't drink when you were working,' he said accusingly.

Startled, Jessamy sprang to her feet, knocking over her glass of lager.

'It's all right, I'm not getting at you. I'm sure you have everything under control.' His words were conciliating but his tone was still angry, as if he *minded* finding her here with Barry and apparently on good terms with him again, Jessamy thought in some confusion.

'I'll have to see to the vegetables if the others are coming back,' she said, excusing herself, but he followed her through into the galley.

'Barry's not been bothering you again, has he?' He gripped her arm.

Jessamy shivered, steeling herself against the treacherous flood of feeling even such a rough touch aroused. 'No, he's not been bothering me,' she said coldly.

He dropped her arm, but his grey eyes still raked her face searchingly and for once Jessamy wasn't sorry for Bianca's interruption.

'Darling, I don't know why this kitchen has such a fatal fascination for you.' The pretended innocence didn't quite disguise the waspish tone. 'I'm sure Jessamy would prefer not to have you under her feet holding her up. And *I* would prefer not to have to wait too much longer for my lunch.'

'It's ready when you are, Miss Mortimer,' said

Jessamy, picking up the tureen of cold consommé to take through to the dining room.

The sun came out while they were having lunch and as they cruised on that afternoon the guests were able to sit out on the well deck. But as Jessamy served afternoon tea, Barry called to warn them they were approaching a tunnel.

Bianca squealed with excitement and they all watched the black hole in the side of the hill into which the canal disappeared slowly coming nearer. Just as the blackness was about to envelop them Barry switched on the boat headlamp and Luke turned the light on in the stateroom.

'Oh no . . .' Bianca protested. 'Switch it off again, Luke. It's much more thrilling going through in the dark.'

Luke did as she asked and there was suddenly nothing but the pale shaft of the headlamp gleaming on the few feet of wet wall just ahead of the boat. Bianca made a great play of being frightened, clinging to Luke and squealing.

Jessamy stood rigid, clutching the back of a chair, perspiration starting from every pore of her body as she fought down the panic. If there was one thing she was afraid of it was the claustrophobic feeling of being buried alive underground.

She strained her eyes ahead, trying to pierce the darkness, praying for that blob of light that would put an end to this torture. At last she thought she saw it, just a pinprick but definitely getting larger, then Barry throttled back to dead slow as the light turned out to be the headlamp of another boat approaching them. As it passed with much shouting and waving from the occupants the darkness seemed to close in even more absolutely.

The boat picked up speed again, but the tunnel seemed to go on interminably, as if they were doomed forever to travel through this Stygian darkness. Jessamy could almost feel the hundreds of tons of rock and earth above pressing down on her and felt sure she was going to disgrace herself and faint away on the stateroom carpet.

Then, when she was almost at the end of her endurance, an egg-shaped light appeared in front, growing steadily larger. Fighting for control over her hysterical panic, she willed the boat towards it, and as they at last broke into the bright sunlight she couldn't hold back the gasp of relief as she was able to fill her lungs with air.

'Jessamy, are you all right?'

She was aware of Luke's shocked concern and his arm suddenly around her shoulders, but she was quite incapable of speaking as white and shaking, she still felt she couldn't get enough air into her starved lungs.

'Poor kid—it's claustrophobia.' Minnie too was on her feet beside her. 'Get her out on deck an' pour some brandy down 'er.'

She tried to walk, but her legs wouldn't seem to obey her, so Luke picked her up bodily and carried her outside, placing her gently on the bench and sitting beside her, his arm still holding her close. Desmond Britton thrust a brandy glass into her hand, but she was shaking too much to hold it to her lips and Luke had to help her, talking soothingly all the time. The glass rattled against her teeth as he coaxed her to take a sip and the burning liquid made her cough.

Everyone hovered round in concern, everyone that is except Bianca who looked thunderous. 'She's putting it on to gain attention,' she said spitefully.

Luke quelled her with a glance. 'It wouldn't have happened if I hadn't pandered to your whim and put the light out,' he said coldly, then he shook Jessamy gently. 'Why didn't you tell me, you little idiot, instead of suffering in silence? Come on, take another sip of this . . .'

She tried to shake her head, but he insisted, and as more of the burning liquid slid down her throat it did seem to steady her. Gradually the shaking subsided and her breathing returned to normal. 'I—I'm terribly sorry,' she said weakly, feeling very foolish as everyone still stared at her. 'I—I'm all right now, really . . .' She tried to stand, but Luke held her down on the seat.

'Now take it easy. There's no reason to go rushing off. Just sit here for a while and relax.' And with his arm still holding her comfortingly close, indeed she was glad to obey him.

'What you need is a cuppa tea,' Minnie said briskly. 'This in 'ere's gone cold. I'll pop an' make a fresh pot.'

'No, really,' Jessamy protested. 'You needn't go to all that trouble.'

'Get away with you! I'm not too proud to put a kettle on.' The little woman bustled off.

By the time they had found a pleasant mooring place for the night and it was time for Jessamy to prepare dinner she was fully recovered, but she still felt very selfconscious about her lapse, wondering uneasily if the other guests believed Bianca's jibe that it had all been put on to gain Luke's attention.

They had moored on the fringes of a small market town and when Jessamy had finished clearing up after dinner she heard Bianca suggest to Luke that they should go for a stroll.

'Good idea,' Luke agreed, and Jessamy was disturbed by the strength of the pang she felt as she thought of the two going off together. But then he said, 'What about you, Minnie? Like to see a bit of civilisation? You too, Jessamy. A stroll in the open air is just what you need after your nasty experience this afternoon.'

In the end they all decided to go, which was quite

obviously not what Bianca had had in mind, by the way she flounced off angrily to fetch her jacket.

Although Barry had reverted to his former platonic friendliness when they talked at lunch time, Jessamy felt she couldn't rely on that lasting if she found herself alone with him, so she stuck close to Minnie Asher, whom she found a very entertaining companion anyway. Bianca would have hurried Luke on away from the rest of the group, but he kept hanging back, measuring his pace to the elderly woman's, and when Bianca tried to monopolise him, kept turning to include Minnie and Jessamy in their conversation.

Luke was only being polite, of course. After all, on this trip he was the overall host as all the guests were there by his specific invitation, but it was obvious Bianca didn't feel he had responsibilities towards anyone but herself, and she was getting more uptight by the minute at having her plans to get Luke to herself thwarted.

It was quite a sizeable town, though on a Sunday evening there were few people about. 'It might be an idea to stock up on your stores here tomorrow, Jessamy,' Luke suggested.

'I could.' She was casting a professional eye over a surprisingly well stocked delicatessen. 'Though I wouldn't want to hold everyone up while I come shopping. I shan't be desperate for stores for another day or so.'

'Make out a list of everything you need and let me have it first thing in the morning,' he said easily. 'If I skip breakfast I can be back by the time the rest of you have finished gorging.'

'Luke, it's not *your* job to act as her lackey,' Bianca said furiously.

'Your vocabulary is beginning to sound as if it's been culled from the pages of a bad historical novel,' Luke retorted. 'First galley slaves and now lackeys—It's *my* job, Bianca, to make sure *all* my guests enjoy this trip, and if that means me having to do a bit of shopping, so be it.'

'If—if you really don't mind, Luke——' Jessamy said uncomfortably, aware of the glance of pure venom the other girl was shooting in her direction, and that Bianca was blaming her for the set-down.

'Look what I've got!'

Jessamy had made the beds and tidied up *Hyacinth* and was back in the galley washing up the breakfast things when Luke burst in, opening one of his many packages and thrusting it under her nose.

'Trout!' She gazed at the silvery fish, already beginning to imagine how they would look grilled and sprinkled with flaked almonds. 'And really fresh too.'

'Just being unloaded from the back of a car when I got to the fishmongers.' He grinned. 'Could be they were poached from someone's trout stream over the weekend, but who am I to ask questions? Make a tasty lunch.'

'Indeed they will,' she gloated, thinking that this would be a meal Desmond Britton could write about.

Luke laughed softly. 'The look on your face, Jessamy! A lot of girls wouldn't look as happy if I'd given them diamonds.'

Jessamy laughed too, but the look on *his* face as he said it started a strange fluttering in her heart.

The morning sped by. Barry had already said they would stop this side of a set of locks he had originally intended to get through before mooring for lunch, as they'd had a slightly delayed start waiting for Luke to get back from his shopping trip. So when they had almost reached the spot, Jessamy put her precious trout under the grill. Right on cue the boat slowed down and stopped, and Barry passed through the galley on his way to the stateroom.

But a few moments later he was back. 'They've

decided to wait for lunch till we're through the lock after all,' he reported. 'And as they're all busy, you'll have to open the gates for me, Jess.'

'But I've already got the lunch on,' she protested in dismay.

He shrugged. 'Boss's orders.'

Busy! she thought crossly. *She* was the only busy one around here.

'It's only three gates, Jess,' Barry urged. 'It won't take long.'

'Oh—all right.' She took off her apron and very carefully turned the grill down to the lowest heat, then taking the windlass she sprang on to the towpath and went to open the first lock gate. While she closed the third after him, Barry drove a little farther to moor well out of the way of other boats wanting to use the lock, leaving Jessamy to follow on foot.

He was busy with the mooring ropes when she jumped back on board, so he didn't hear her gasp of dismay as she opened the door into the galley and found the room full of acrid black smoke. Choking, she groped blindly to the grill and could hardly believe her eyes when she found it burning away full blast and the eight beautiful trout that should have graced the table in a few minutes nothing but charred, smoking cinders. Turning off the gas, she flung open the windows, coughing and spluttering as she tried to fan the awful black smoke outside.

'I *knew* I gotta whiff of somethin' burnin'!' Minnie Asher burst into the galley, closely followed by Luke.

'Jessamy! What's happened?' In a bound he was by her side.

'The trout—oh, the trout——' she mourned, holding the red-hot grill pan in a gloved hand.

'Good grief! I thought you were supposed to be an experienced cook,' Luke shouted angrily. 'A complete beginner could have done better than that!'

The meal that was to have prompted Desmond Britton to write a glowing report about their hotel-boat enterprise for the newspapers was in ruins, and as if that wasn't bad enough, Luke was putting all the blame on her.

'I am,' she shouted back, 'but not even the chef at Buckingham Palace could do his best when he's told to act as cabin boy as well. *You* gave the order to go on through the locks. Surely it wouldn't have hurt you to have opened the gates for Barry instead of expecting me to do it?'

His face froze at her accusation. 'You've never started cooking before until we'd moored,' he said coldly.

'No, but this time I did because we were running late. And anyway, I'd been told we were stopping the *other* side of the locks.' Jessamy's anger was as hot as his was cold.

Not by a muscle did Luke betray the possibility that *he* might bear some blame for this disaster. 'And it never occurred to you to turn the grill off before you left it?'

'I did. At least, I turned it down as far as it would go without blowing out.' Her cheeks burned at the injustice of his anger.

'You mean you *thought* you did,' he sneered. 'They never reached that state under a low grill.'

'No, they didn't. When I got back the grill had been turned up full blast.'

"And who do you think did that? The gremlins? It's no good trying to make excuses for your own negligence, Jessamy. Criminal negligence. People's lives could have been lost if the boat had gone up in flames,' His cold voice lashed her as he snatched the grill pan from her and threw the rapidly cooling remains of the trout into the waste bin. 'I don't want anything like this to happen *ever* again. Now you'd better do something about getting together an alternative lunch for our guests. I suggest some of the cold meats I bought this morning, with salad.' He turned on his heel and marched out.

'Phew! Can't 'alf throw 'is weight about when 'e's riled,' Minnie commented. 'Never mind, ducks. Don't take it too 'ard.'

'But I *did* turn that grill down,' Jessamy insisted, tears of indignation and mortification swimming in her eyes. 'I *know* I did. I even stood by it a few moments to make sure it didn't go out, so I'm certain I didn't turn it up by mistake.'

Minnie pursed her lips thoughtfully. 'Well, there's only one person left the room while we was goin' through them locks—Bianca. I *thought* she was goin' to the loo——'

'Bianca!' It figured, Jessamy thought angrily, re-membering the venom in the other girl's eyes the previous night. She'd wanted Luke to herself and she'd blamed Jessamy for not getting her way. This was her revenge, then, a deliberate act to make Luke think badly of the girl she considered had been taking too much of his attention away from Bianca herself.

'You don't want to let 'er get away with it, ducks. You go on in there and split on 'er,' Minnie urged. 'I'll back you up.'

'No.' Jessamy drew herself up proudly. If Luke couldn't trust her integrity, if he couldn't accept her word, then he could think what he liked. He wouldn't believe her anyway, not when Bianca denied it, as she certainly would. 'And I'd rather you didn't mention your suspicions either, Minnie. Not to anyone.' She was remembering all too clearly Luke's previous warning when he'd accused her of encouraging Minnie to gossip.


## CHAPTER EIGHT

FOR the next few days the cruise proceeded smoothly without any more disasters or emotional traumas, mostly, Jessamy suspected, because Bianca was all sunny smiles and sweet innocent delight, having recaptured Luke's attention solely to herself.

Ever since his stinging reproof over the burnt trout, Jessamy had avoided him as much as possible, even persuading Barry to take him his early morning tea, and Desmond Britton's as well, in case their employer should feel he had been singled out. Whenever it was unavoidable to have contact with him she treated him with strict formality and tried not to let his reciprocal coldness hurt. Bianca made no attempt to hide her triumph at causing the rift between them, at least in front of Jessamy.

Even so, Jessamy would lie awake long into the night thinking of Bianca queening it in her appropriated double cabin and wondering if Luke was making the most of her near proximity.

At the various stopping places along the way they had refuelled the boat, taken on fresh water, exchanged empty cylinders of bottled gas for full ones and restocked the stores, though Jessamy had been very careful to do the shopping herself and not impose on Luke again.

It was Wednesday evening when they moored near Leamington Spa. Luke had instructed Jessamy that morning not to prepare an evening meal as he had arranged for them all to eat ashore. It was for occasions like this that he had equipped her with the three beautiful evening dresses, but the coldness that still existed between them and her burning sense of injustice at his undeserved anger took away all pleasure in the prospect of wearing one of them.

For two pins, she thought, she would plead a headache and not go. But she knew that would be childish behaviour, and anyway, who was she trying to hurt? With Bianca on his arm he wouldn't even notice her absence.

Usually with dinner to cook her evening ablutions

had to be perfunctory, but tonight, without that chore, she decided she would make good use of the unaccustomed leisure. As soon as the boat was moored and while everyone else was having a quick sundowner in the bar, she slipped away to *Hyacinth* to be the first to use the shower, washing her hair till it squeaked, then rubbing it until it was nearly dry before putting it up on rollers.

So used was she to hurrying from one task to another she had to school herself to take her time and to enjoy having nothing else to do for once except make herself look attractive. After all, she *had* managed to make herself look pretty good the night Luke had taken her to dine at the Sun, she thought, and she intended to do it again. Only this time she wasn't going to let him melt her like hot chocolate. This time she intended to stay cool and aloof.

While her hair was drying she tried each of the three new dresses on in turn, twirling critically before the mirror and finally deciding on the fine black wool again. She hadn't had time for sunbathing like Bianca so she had no golden tan to flaunt, and the long sleeves meant she wouldn't need a wrap as the evening got cooler. Besides, she thought the black was better suited to the icy image she was determined to assume.

As she had been busy with her hair she had heard the other guests coming back to *Hyacinth* to change. She heard too—as she was sure she was meant to—Bianca say, 'Luke darling, I do think it's a bit much having to take the *staff* out with us tonight.' She hadn't caught Luke's reply.

So now dressed, perfumed, her face made up to the utmost of her skill, her shining fair hair in a more sophisticated style than she had ever attempted before, she waited until she was sure everyone had gone back to the stateroom. And while she waited she practised a cool, aloof expression in the mirror. For the first time in her life Jessamy meant to make an Entrance.

The last footsteps and voices died away and *Hyacinth* was silent. She waited another couple of minutes, watching the seconds tick by on her travelling clock, then stood up and strolled out of her cabin as if she had all the time in the world. The stateroom was full of laughter and chatter as she passed it on the towpath and for just a moment she felt desperately nervous. But lifting her head high and taking a deep breath, she stepped delicately down on to the well deck in her high heels and paused in the doorway.

The kind of hush she had sometimes read about but never experienced fell as one after the other they each forgot what they were saying and stared.

'Good evening,' she said coolly, noticing Minnie's approving grin, Brad's ogling leer and his wife's frozen hostility. Barry, unfamiliar and ill at ease in a black dinner jacket, looked positively stupefied at the transformation of his one-time barmaid, but it was the stunned, disbelieving expression on Bianca's face that gave her the most satisfaction.

At last, reluctant but unable to prevent herself, she looked at Luke. She had half hoped to see the same stunned expression on *his* face, but she had also steeled herself against his indifference. What she hadn't expected was to see his mouth curving into a half smile and his eyes dancing with amusement!

'Ah, Jessamy——' He took her hand and drew her into the room. 'The cars are not due for another ten minutes, so you've time for a drink. What will you have?'

Jessamy would have liked fruit juice, but she didn't want to spoil the impression she'd made. 'A Martini, please,' she said calmly. 'Very dry.'

When she got it she found it almost undrinkable, the dryness contracting her facial muscles into a grimace as if she was sucking lemons. Aware of Luke's sardonically raised eyebrow, she hastily put her glass down on a table,

and was very relieved when a toot from the bridge near
where they were moored signalled the arrival of the two
large cars Luke had arranged to pick them up.

As they all trooped out, Minnie Asher managed to
whisper hoarsely in her ear, 'Good fer you, ducks! Put
Madam's nose out o' joint proper, you 'ave!' But
Minnie was mistaken if she thought Jessamy held all the
cards. Bianca neatly arranged it so she, Luke and
Minnie sat together in the back of one car while
Jessamy had to travel in front beside the driver.

The restaurant Luke had chosen was palatial, almost
a stately home that had been turned into a hotel,
standing in beautiful grounds that even included a lake.
Bianca sailed in as if this kind of background was her
natural habitat, but Jessamy tried not to look too
overawed by all the splendour.

A four-piece band played discreetly while they ate,
though as more and more people got up to dance they
threw discretion to the winds and played livelier
numbers. Time and time again Bianca dragged Luke to
his feet and on to the dance floor while Jessamy had to
suffer Barry's clumsy, embarrassed shuffle, Brad's hot,
pawing clutch while his wife's eyes pursued them, and
being trundled round the floor by Desmond Britton for
all the world as if she was a perambulator.

She kept telling herself she did *not* want Luke to ask
her to dance, and if he did, she would refuse him coldly.
But when, after returning Bianca to her seat, instead of
sitting down himself he immediately came round the
table and took her hand, she found herself rising to her
feet without a murmur of protest.

'I don't mind Bianca snatching all those wild modern
dances, but she's not having this smoochy number,' he
whispered in her ear, and as his arm clasped her waist
firmly her traitorous body wanted to melt against his.
But she was determined tonight to deny his power over
her and she held herself stiffly away from him.

'I won't bite, you know.' He eyed her quizzically as she circled the floor as stiff as a wooden soldier.

'That's a debatable point.' She kept up her cool front, thought it was very trying on her will power, and the heavy panelled, ornately ceilinged room seemed stifling.

'You *can't* be as cool as you look, and I certainly could do with some air.' Very skilfully and without breaking his step he steered her through a door and out into the garden.

Her heart began to beat very fast. 'I don't really think—I mean, they'll wonder where we've gone.' She tried to hang back.

'Let them wonder,' he said carelessly. 'Come on, I want to show you the beautiful gardens.' Taking her hand, he hurried her across the lawn before she could resist.

It was almost dark, but beyond the light spilling out from the windows on to the grass, the lake gleamed palely. Luke made for it, slowing down to a stroll. Night-scented stock perfumed the air and the music the band was playing was sweetened by distance. There was no moon, but as they reached the lake they saw distinctly the ghostly shapes of two swans floating by.

'Romantic, wouldn't you say?' Luke stopped and turned to face her.

Too damned romantic by half, and he knew it, Jessamy thought, gritting her teeth. 'If you like that sort of thing.' She started to stroll on, but he caught her wrist.

'You don't have to keep on punishing me for tearing a strip off you,' he said softly. 'Forgive and forget?' His mouth captured hers gently and his arms drew her to him.

She almost surrendered to the languorous fire his touch aroused. Only sheer will power helped her to fight her treacherous senses and hold herself back.

He lifted his head. 'Am I losing my touch?'

'Do you *have* to be so insulting?' Her voice shook

with cold fury at the sheer arrogance of the man.

His eyes widened. 'I didn't notice you feeling insulted when I kissed you before. In fact I thought——'

'That I was easy?' Jessamy broke in fiercely. 'I would say I'm sorry to disappoint you, but it wouldn't be true. I'm not a *bit* sorry. Maybe judged by the circles *you* move in I'm a prude, so you'd better stick to your own kind when you're looking for a bit on the side!'

His hand gripped her wrist like a vice. 'I think you'd better explain that remark.'

'Explain?' She stood before him quivering with outrage. 'I need to explain? All right. In words of one syllable—I can feel nothing but contempt for a man who brings his girl-friend along on a fortnight's holiday and then spends half his time trying to seduce someone else!'

His grip on her wrist tightened painfully. 'Bianca . . .' His voice was soft, almost as if he was talking to himself. 'I'm beginning to feel sorry I asked her along.'

'I'm not,' Jessamy retorted instantly. 'At least it's made me see what you're really like—selfish and callous—otherwise I might have actually believed . . .' her voice ended on a sob.

'You might have believed what? That I'm as attracted to you as you are to me, however hard you try to pretend differently?' The vice-like grip on her wrist was relaxed and his hand slid caressingly up her arm to her shoulder, drawing her closer. But though she was no longer a prisoner she was rooted to the spot by the unexpected tenderness in his voice. 'Oh, Jessamy, I'm making an awful mess of things, aren't I?'

Jessamy closed her eyes and swayed slightly. 'Bianca——' she said in a strangled voice.

'Has nothing whatever to do with the way I feel about you.' His hand lay warm on her neck and his thumb stroked her cheek. 'Bianca's an old friend. I asked her along because she's had a bad time recently and I wanted to cheer her up. But she doesn't own me, even if sometimes she likes to think she does.' This last remark was made with a rueful dryness.

No man had ever had such a devastating effect on her before, such an irresistible pull of attraction. Against her better judgement, against all her instincts for self-preservation, she found herself desperately wanting to believe him. 'Luke——'

She was trembling violently and he pulled her into his arms, making no attempt to kiss her or play on her passion, just holding her gently and comfortingly. 'Jessamy, can't you begin to trust me? Couldn't we spend the rest of this trip getting to know each other without you suspecting my every word and action?'

She could feel his heart beating steadily against her breast and it felt so right lying there, gently cradled in his arms that she promised shakily, 'All right—I'll try.'

The party broke up almost immediately when they finally returned to their table. Bianca barely concealed her livid jealousy as she possessively seized Luke's arm, and Barry's look of hurt misery filled Jessamy with a crushing guilt as she realised his jealousy now had some foundation.

'I'd never have believed you could be so disloyal, Jess,' he muttered as they made their way back to the cars. 'It's bad enough having to watch you chasing after another man, but to see you getting the hots for Luke Monro—the man who cheated me and took over my business . . .'

Jessamy suddenly felt icy cold. She had promised Luke she would trust him, completely forgetting the very good reasons she had for *dis*trusting him. He'd sounded absolutely sincere by the lake tonight, but wasn't he a man accustomed to getting his own way? And hadn't he already proved how unscrupulous he could be in getting what he wanted? He'd told her openly at the beginning of this trip that he meant to use the time changing her low opinion of him.

Guilt, confusion and wretchedness kept her awake long into the night and lay in wait for her the moment she opened her eyes in the morning.

When she went to the galley to prepare the early morning tea her heart turned over to find Luke already there at the stove boiling the first kettle. He looked so overwhelmingly attractive and had such a light of eagerness in his dark eyes it was all she could do to stop herself falling into his arms. She had to remind herself this was all an act for him, that Luke was an utterly unscrupulous man who was laying siege to her for some devious reason of his own—perhaps to punish her for her earlier straight-from-the-shoulder remarks on his character. It was important that she kept her head and let him see she hadn't been taken in.

'Good morning,' she said coolly. 'It's kind of you to come and help, but I can manage perfectly well on my own, thank you.'

The eagerness faded from his expression and his jaw tightened. 'What sort of a greeting is that, when I got up early so we could have a little time alone together?'

'I didn't ask you to.' The cups rattled in her nervous hands as she set them out.

He looked baffled. 'Jessamy! Last night——'

'Last night I was suffering from too much wine and moonlight,' she interrupted quickly. 'A fatal combination in the company of a man as experienced as you. In the cold light of morning I realise——'

She broke off as he advanced on her until he had her penned against the wall and she gave a little moan of fright as his angry face drew inexorably nearer. She tried to fend him off, but she might as well have been flapping her hands at a maddened bull. He seized her roughly and his kiss was intended to hurt with its bruising pressure and utter lack of tenderness.

She should have felt humiliated by the punishing assault, but instead a strange and shaming excitement stirred in her, firing her senses, weakening her resistance until she was no longer trying to push him away but was surrendering to his superior strength with a shivering, shuddering delight.

At last he drew back and she would have fallen had she not still been clinging round his neck. 'And in the cold light of morning, Jessamy?' he said mockingly, his eyes feasting on her mouth that felt swollen and tingling from his ruthless possession. 'You can't blame the wine and the moonlight now. Or are you still going to try to deny you want me as much as I want you?'

'Luke——' A lock of hair had fallen on to his brow, breaking the strong, dark V of his hairline. Tentatively she brushed it back, her mouth trembling.

'You really are the most capricious, exasperating, aggravating and totally unforgettable girl I've ever met,' he said softly, bending his head to her neck and running tiny hot kisses along a sensitive line that made her gasp and arch her body towards him, begging for more.

'It's perhaps as well we don't have the opportunity to be alone together for long,' he said huskily when at last they broke apart for breath. 'You make it damned hard for a man to keep control of himself.'

It was then that a movement out on the rear deck caught her eye and Jessamy realised Barry stood there staring at them. With a warning look at Luke she pulled away from him and turned to the stove where the boiling kettle was filling the galley with steam. Embarrassed colour burned her cheeks as she wondered how long Barry had been watching them and how much he'd heard.

That he had seen and heard most of what had passed between them became apparent at lunchtime when they moored beside another waterside inn. The guests went off to stretch their legs in fresh surroundings, promising not to be long, and though Luke was reluctant to join them, Bianca naturally demanded his comapny.

There wasn't a great deal for Jessamy to do as she

had decided earlier to put on a cold table, knowing Luke wanted this lunchtime stop to be as brief as possible in order to reach Stratford-on-Avon by nightfall. When everything was done she went out on to the rear deck for a few minutes, expecting to be alone, only to find Barry waiting for her, hunched on the bench beside the tiller. She hesitated in the doorway, the brooding look on his face making her wary.

'You're in love with him, aren't you?' he said flatly. 'You might as well admit it. I saw you together, remember—heard what you said.'

Jessamy moistened suddenly dry lips. She hadn't dared to examine the overwhelming feelings she had for Luke before, but she knew with a sudden flash of clarity that it was true. 'Yes, I love him,' she said softly.

He turned his head away. 'How you can be such a fool . . .'

'Barry, I'm sorry.' She sat down beside him and took the hand that was clenched into a fist on the bench at his side. 'I know all the arguments against it, and I know you feel it's disloyal of me to feel the way I do. He's arrogant, ruthless, even unscrupulous. I didn't *want* it to happen, but it did.'

He turned and looked at her. 'He'll never marry you, you know.'

It was like a cold wind from the arctic blowing over her. Luke had talked about wanting, never about love, and certainly not about marriage. She sighed heavily. 'You're probably right. We belong to entirely different worlds. If he ever does get married it won't be to someone like me who's momentarily caught his fancy, it'll be someone from his own world, someone with money and position.' Someone like Bianca, she thought, a knife twisting in her heart.

'But it doesn't seem to make any difference,' she said helplessly, looking at Barry with more sympathy than she'd felt for him for some time. 'Any more than knowing I shall never marry you seems to have made any difference to *you*.'

His clenched fist relaxed beneath her hand. He moved his arm and put it round her shoulders. 'I reckon fate's played a dirty trick on both of us, love,' he said wryly.

She relaxed against him, letting her head droop on to his shoulder, agreeing with him sadly and feeling that at last there was real understanding between them.

'Oh, how cosy! Luke, *don't* they look cosy together?'

Bianca's voice startled Jessamy so much she jumped as if she'd been stung and guilty colour rose in her cheeks as the rest of the party stared hard. 'The lunch is all ready . . .' she babbled, catching sight of the tight set of Luke's jaw. Scrambling through the door of the galley, she felt as if she'd been caught out doing something wrong.

Luke was rather quiet as she served lunch and Jessamy was afraid her stupidly guilty reaction at being caught with Barry's arm around her had given him the wrong impression. Of course she would be able to explain to him how innocent it had all been.

But somehow the opportunity never arose. Immediately after lunch they moved off again. As she worked in the galley, washing up and making preparations for the evening meal, she hoped Luke might come through and talk to her so she could put things right between them, but he didn't. There were too many people around when she served the tea to say the things she wanted to say, and afterwards he was deep in conversation with Desmond Britton.

They sailed on much later than usual because Luke was determined they should have a full day in Stratford on the Saturday. With everything done that had to be done until she could actually start cooking, Jessamy sat with the guests in the stateroom rather than make things look worse by joining Barry on the rear deck.

Luke was still talking to Desmond and Bianca prowled restlessly. When her obvious dissatisfaction made no impression on Luke, Bianca abruptly disappeared.

Remembering the incident of the grill being mysteriously turned up high, Jessamy was immediately suspicious, and after a few moments, followed quietly to see what the girl was up to. The dining room and the galley were empty and she was puzzled, until she heard Bianca's trilling laughter and through the glass panel in the door saw to her astonishment that the beautiful and status conscious guest was sitting on the bench seat of the rear deck laughing up at Barry as he stood at the tiller.

At last the rooftops of Stratford-on-Avon came into view. They found a pleasant spot to moor and Jessamy was able to begin the dinner. They were so late that guests had begun to retire to their cabins while she was still clearing up the galley. Luke and Desmond Britton were the only ones remaining in the stateroom, and although she still longed to talk to Luke to eradicate the guilty impression she had given when he'd surprised her with Barry, she could see they wouldn't welcome her interruption, so she said goodnight and tiredly walked along the towpath to *Hyacinth*. It would have to wait till morning now. Perhaps Luke would get up early to help her again.

She thought Bianca had already retired to bed, so she was surprised to see her, still fully dressed, hovering near the gangway.

'Oh, Jessamy, I hoped you wouldn't be long,' she said in an urgent whisper. 'Barry's not feeling at all well. I've sent him to his cabin and he *says* he'll be all right by morning, but——' She shook her head worriedly. 'He really did look rotten. Do you think——'

'I'll go and look at him,' Jessamy said at once, alarmed.

The crew's cabin which Barry occupied was right in the stern of *Hyacinth*, apart from the guests' cabins and having its own separate entrance from the tiny stern deck. Suspecting nothing, she scrambled up and opened the door. The light was still on and Barry lay on the rumpled double bed, his eyes closed.

'Barry! Bianca says you're ill. What is it?' She leaned over him, putting her hand to his brow to see if he was running a temperature. With a speed that took her completely by surprise his arms reached up and grabbed her, pulling her down on the bed.

For a couple of moments she was too stunned to struggle, but when he rolled over so he was lying on top of her, pinning her down, panic rose up and she started to kick, trying to shake him off.

'Don't fight me, Jess. Relax ... just relax,' Barry gasped hoarsely, his pale eyes alight with excitement.

'Have you gone mad!' She could hardly breathe with his weight crushing her. 'Barry—for pity's sake!'

He stopped her protests by fastening his mouth on hers. She writhed and twisted, trying to escape, but it only seemed to excite him more. Roughly he ripped open her lacy shirt and began kissing the cleft between her breasts. She had actually taken a deep breath to scream when the door opened.

'Jessamy!' Luke's face was haggard with shock and disbelief.

Barry released her at once, swinging his legs to the floor and glowering at Luke with a mixture of triumph and resentment. But Jessamy was only aware of Luke's hard eyes fixed on her accusingly as she struggled off Barry's bed, trying to pull her torn shirt around her.

'Luke! I'm sorry, but it's not——' she began desperately, but he gave her no chance to explain.

'It's I who owe *you* the apology.' His face was like carved granite. 'I shouldn't have come here, but when Bianca said she'd seen you sneaking into Barry's cabin I didn't believe her. I only wanted to prove her wrong. Please accept my apologies for the interruption.' The door clicked with a terrible finality behind him.

'Bianca!' White-faced and shaking Jessamy stared at Barry, who at least had the grace to look sheepish. 'You set this up between the pair of you, didn't you?' she accused. 'This afternoon when she was suddenly so matey with you. And tonight—getting me in here, telling me you were ill. I should have *known* she had an ulterior motive!'

His glance slid away in tacit admission of guilt and he stared silently at the floor.

'I suppose I shouldn't be surprised at Bianca playing such a trick,' she said bitterly. 'But *you*! I thought you were my friend!'

'I only agreed because I thought it might cure you of that silly infatuation for Monro,' he mumbled.

'Infatuation! How dare you suppose it was only infatuation?' she blazed at him. 'I'll never forgive you for this, Barry! Don't ever touch me or come near me again!' Holding her tattered shirt together to cover herself, she opened the door.

Barry leapt to his feet. 'Jess, I only did it for us,' he pleaded. 'You know how much I love you.'

'Oh no, you didn't, Barry,' she said quietly, looking at him with withering scorn. 'Love? You don't know the meaning of the word. If you'd had the slightest genuine feeling for me you could never have played such a low, despicable trick!'

Sheer anger kept her going until she reached her own cabin and then her legs collapsed beneath her and she fell on to her bed, sobbing as if her heart would break.

# CHAPTER NINE

OF course Luke wasn't in the galley early the next morning, and neither did Barry turn up to help her deliver the trays to the cabins. Barry's defection was a relief, because Jessamy didn't know if she could bring herself to be civil to him, though it did mean she would be forced to take Luke's tray in to him herself.

Perhaps he would have cooled down by this morning and be prepared to listen to her explanation of the apparently damning events last night. So it was with a nervous hope that she tapped on his door. But before she could turn the knob the door was snatched open and a stony-faced Luke took the tray from her wordlessly and shut the door in her face.

For a few moments she stood there stunned and deeply hurt, before anger came to her rescue. All right, so he had found her in a very compromising situation, but surely if he felt anything for her at all— as he claimed he did—he would at least have wanted to hear *her* side of the story. Didn't the fact that it had been Bianca who'd told him she would be found in Barry's cabin make him even a *little* suspicious? Apparently not. He was too ready to think the worst of her to even suspect he'd been duped.

Pride stiffened her backbone. A man who could so easily be manipulated by a scheming woman like Bianca was contemptible. Not by the flicker of an eyelash would she betray how much his lack of trust in her integrity had hurt her.

Schooling her features to impassivity, she took in Bianca's tray. The girl lolled on her pillows, her curly hair tumbled, avid curiosity in her dark eyes as she watched Jessamy cross the cabin and put the tray beside her.

'I hear Barry made a very speedy recovery last night,' she said slyly, a smile curving her full mouth.

Jessamy's clenched hands were hidden in the folds of her skirt as she looked down at the girl who lay there like a satisfied cat full of stolen cream, and she fought back the bitter accusation that rose to her tongue. 'I found him perfectly fit,' she said remotely. 'Good morning.' The baffled look on Bianca's face gave her some satisfaction before she closed the door on it.

But as she returned to *Tiger Lily* her shoulders slumped. She might have puzzled Bianca for the time being, but it wouldn't be long before the girl learned just how well her underhand trick had worked. She would only have to take one look at Luke's stony face.

That was the worst day of Jessamy's life. At breakfast Luke was every bit as granite-faced as she had feared, until everyone—except Bianca—seemed infected by his foul mood.

Everyone could do their own thing today, he told them in a flat voice. Lunch would be served on the boat for anyone who wanted it—he didn't even glance at Jessamy as he said it—but there was no compulsion to come back if they'd rather make their own arrangements in the town. A rather more substantial tea than usual would be ready on the boat at half past four, to take guests through until the late supper he had booked at a local restaurant after the performance at the Royal Shakespeare Theatre, for which he had tickets for everyone.

'And what are *we* doing today, darling?' Bianca asked eagerly, linking her arm in his as he rose from the table.

'I'm sorry, you'll have to amuse yourself for once,' he said shortly. 'I have business to attend to.'

Jessamy wouldn't have been human if she hadn't

enjoyed the disappointed chagrin on Bianca's face as
Luke walked stiff-backed away from the boat.

'I suppose you told him——' she hissed venomously
at Jessamy.

Jessamy looked at her with assumed puzzlement.
'Told him? Told him what?' At least that had given her
something to wonder about, she thought sourly as she
watched Bianca flounce off and attach herself to
Desmond Britton.

''Ow about you, ducks?' Minnie Asher asked as
Jessamy began to clear the breakfast table. 'Want to
come along of us?' She had struck up quite a friendship
with Brad and Amy Francis, and Amy looked alarmed
at Minnie's invitation until Jessamy shook her head.

'Thanks, Minnie, but I have a lot of stores to get this
morning and you won't want to waste your time
hanging around the shops when there's so much else to
see.'

While she was clearing up on the boat she was aware
that Barry was hanging about even after he had finished
filling the freshwater tanks and had switched the
cylinders of bottled gas for full ones, and as she set off
with her shopping bags he came after her. 'Jess, you'll
need me to help you carry all that stuff back.'

'Thank you, but I can manage.' Her voice was cold
and remote and she stared straight ahead. And when he
persisted in walking along beside her she rounded on
him. 'I told you last night, Barry. I can't bear to have
you anywhere near me!'

His face seemed to crumple and without another
word he turned back to the boat. For a few moments
she stood there looking after him, not liking the bitter,
unforgiving person she seemed to have become. But she
found it too much to forgive the man she had trusted as
a friend and who had betrayed that trust in such a
heartless and distasteful way. Had he cared what misery
he caused her? She walked on.

By the time she returned to the boat weighed down by her heavy shopping bags there was no sign of Barry. She made herself a cup of coffee and sat out on the well deck for a while in the sun, watching the world go by and trying—not very successfully—not to think of Luke. Did he really have business in Stratford? Or had he taken himself off in high dudgeon to be rid of them all?

She closed her eyes, telling herself it didn't matter either way. But behind her eyelids she could still see the shocked disbelief on his face when he had found her in Barry's bed. She supposed coming upon them like that it *could* have looked like passion and not the desperate fight it had really been. Tears squeezed between her tightly closed eyelids. If only it didn't hurt so much, having him think so badly of her!

Not knowing how many guests to expect back for lunch, she set out a cold table in the dining room, but by half past one it was apparent none of them meant to return, so she put it all back in the refrigerator. The afternoon stretched empty and lonely in front of her, three hours to fill before she had to be back to serve tea. Although she had little enthusiasm for it now, she supposed she ought to see something of Stratford while she was here.

It was a mistake. She bought a guide book and found her way through the streets of half-timbered buildings that must have changed little since Shakespeare's day, except for the tarmacked road surface and the choking traffic. Shakespeare's birthplace in Henley Street was her first objective, but as she wandered through the rooms, awed by the sheer age of the place—over four hundred years and looking as if it could withstand another four hundred with its sturdy oak beams, its huge brick and stone fireplaces, the stone floors downstairs and the solid oak floors upstairs—she found herself wishing so much she could have shared all this with Luke that it was a physical pain in her chest.

She wished she could have laughed with him when she discovered how very uncomfortable the bed in which the bard was supposed to have been born looked. She wished she could have shared with him her excitement at being able to actually read the signatures Sir Walter Scott and Thomas Carlyle among others had scratched on the window glass in the room.

She wished she could have giggled with him over the spit and great cooking pots in the kitchen and marvelled with him at the ingenuity of the 'baby-minder', a curious device of a swivelling pole between floor and ceiling with a bar projecting from it about two feet from the ground to which the Elizabethan child was strapped so it could run round in a circle without being in danger of falling into the open fire.

From the birthplace she made her way to the ancient Gild Chapel and Grammar School, passing in High Street the beautifully decorated Harvard House, once the home of Katherine Rogers, mother of John Harvard, the founder of Harvard University and now, according to her guide book, the property of the American nation.

In the Grammar School she wished Luke could have shared with her the vision of the doublet-and-hosed young boy huddled over his desk conning his Latin in the high-ceilinged room that rose to a peak under the slates and was criss-crossed with massive supporting beams, and where the diamond-paned windows must often have drawn Will Shakespeare's longing gaze. And beneath the schoolroom in the Gildhall she would have liked Luke too to have imagined that same young boy's excitement as he saw there, perhaps for the very first time in his life, a band of travelling players performing a play.

But there was no one to share this lovely place or her

lively imagination with, and as she sat in the garden of
New Place nearby with its four 'knotts' or beds, each
made up of an intricate, interlacing pattern of flowers
and sweet-smelling herbs, the tears squeezed between
her eyelids again. Useless to tell herself if Luke *had* been
here to share it, so would Bianca, impatiently trying to
drag him elsewhere.

She saw nothing of the others until she returned to
the boat and found Minnie, Brad and Amy sitting out
on the well deck. 'Tea won't be a minute,' she called,
trying to sound bright and carefree but failing
miserably.

Luke was the last to return as everyone else was
tucking hungrily into the tea of thin sandwiches, toasted
muffins and cake.

'Don't you ever do that to me again!' she heard
Bianca hiss at him, sulky and cross after her day in
Desmond Britton's company. 'Leaving me alone like
that. I've had an *awful* day!'

Serve her right too, Jessamy thought with no
compunction. It was Bianca's underhand, vindictive
plotting that had been responsible for so many of the
party's stretched nerves and downright unhappiness
today, so it was only fair that she should take her share.
And it didn't seem to occur to the selfish little madam
that Luke too had had an awful day, if his tired, drawn
face was anything to go by.

As the guests began to drift off to their cabins to
change for the evening, Jessamy cleared away and
began to wash up.

'Leave that and go and get changed or you'll make us
late.' Luke had followed her and she found she was
trembling. It was the first time he had spoken to her
directly since his terrible bitingly sarcastic apology the
previous night and his voice was still curt and angry.

'I—I shan't be coming.' She clutched the edge of the
sink to stop herself trembling, knowing she couldn't sit

there, watching *Romeo and Juliet* of all things! so close and yet so very far from him. 'I'm sure you'll be able to dispose of my ticket at the box office.'

In a stride he had gripped her wrist and whirled her round to face him. 'You'll come whether you like it or not,' he ground out, his eyes blazing. 'This party's falling apart at the seams as it is, without you giving it the *coup de grâce*. You're paid to act as hostess, remember, and highly paid at that. So earn your salary!'

Jessamy cringed under those blazing eyes and the merciless lash of his tongue, then turned and fled, slipping and twisting her ankle as she leapt from the rear deck to the tow path. But she didn't even notice the pain in her greater agony.

That a man who had spoken to her so tenderly by the lake a few nights ago and the man who had looked at her now with such bitter contempt should be one and the same was unbelievable. She fumbled her way to her cabin blinded by tears. How *could* he say such wounding things, implying that she wasn't earning her keep? Shocked and deeply hurt, she fell on to her bed and wept.

But as she began to hear the guests leaving *Hyacinth* she knew she had to try to pull herself together. Luke had meant what he said about her accompanying the party tonight to the theatre, and if she didn't put in an appearance he was quite capable of dragging her along by force.

Washing her face with cold water removed the tear stains but did little to improve her reddened eyes, and there was scant time left to see what cosmetics could do. A touch of eyeshadow helped, but not even the beautiful kingfisher blue silk dress she slipped over her head could restore the colour and sparkle to her quenched eyes. Uncaring, she brushed her hair, leaving it loose on her shoulders, picked up her purse and still feeling sick and shaky, joined the guests in the stateroom.

They walked to the theatre as it was no great distance and on the rough towpath Jessamy began to feel the pain from her twisted ankle. Barry was the only one to notice her difficulty and tried to take her arm but she drew herself away from his distasteful touch. *He* was the one responsible for her awful misery. Bianca, however spiteful her intentions, couldn't have achieved it without his willing connivance. Jessamy felt she could never forgive him.

She was sunk too deep in her misery and too preoccupied by her throbbing ankle to be aware of her surroundings when they reached the world-famous theatre set beside the river Avon, except to notice Luke was seated in the row behind with Bianca, Brad and Amy, and to be relieved that Minnie was sitting between herself and Barry. She did wonder briefly what the little cockney woman would make of Shakespeare, but as the play progressed she could see Minnie was enthralled.

She should have been enthralled herself, she thought unhappily as she watched the star-crossed lovers on stage. And she would have been had she been able to watch it with Luke, before this impenetrable wall of bitterness and anger had reared up between them. Even as she let the poignant poetry of Juliet's lines wash over her: '... *My bounty is as boundless as the sea, my love as deep; the more I give to thee the more I have, for both are infinite ...*' she thought her heart would break, knowing he was sitting right behind her—with Bianca. Her love too ran deep, and though Luke had no use for it, she could no more stem its flow than she could stem the flow of the sea.

At the interval when everyone else got up to stretch their legs, Jessamy remained in her seat, pretending to study her programme. Her ankle was swelling badly now, the straps of her sandals cutting into her flesh, and it was less painful if she kept her weight off it.

At last the performance was over, but she still had to endure the supper party with Bianca flirting archly with Luke on the opposite side of the table. Jessamy could only pick at her food, but she found the wine dulled her pain just a little. Everyone was busy discussing the play and no one seemed to notice she had little to offer to the conversation.

Walking back to the hotel-boats Jessamy could only think longingly of her bed and privacy. The effort of keeping up with the others made the pain in her ankle agonising. She had been trying not to limp, but once they reached the rough ground of the towpath she couldn't help gasping as her ankle turned again.

Luke looked at her sharply. 'Good grief! Your foot's swollen like a balloon! You haven't been walking on it like that all night?'

'It's only a twist.' She tried to brush it off lightly.

'Barry, you might give Jessamy a hand.' Luke's voice was frigid.

'Thank you, but I don't need any help,' she snapped, and walked on, biting her lip to stop herself crying out again.

'Stubborn little fool!' Luke picked her up roughly and strode on with her towards the boat.

There was no tenderness in the arms that held her. She could feel his antagonism like a palpable thing as she huddled there helpless. He squeezed with difficulty through the narrow passageway and dumped her unceremoniously on her bed.

'Take off your pantyhose,' he ordered, and when she protested, 'It's all right, I don't fancy a romp with you right now.' His lip curled contemptuously. 'I'm going to get some ice.'

Jessamy managed to get her sandal off and stripped off her pantyhose. Hopping on her good foot, she crossed to the handbasin and filled it with cold water, then standing on one leg, plunged the swollen foot into it.

'For pity's sake!' Luke exclaimed in exasperation when he came back with the ice and the first aid box. 'Are you *trying* to cripple yourself? Get back on that bed!'

She dried her foot and hobbled back, seething at his heartless bullying.

'You're an accident looking for somewhere to happen,' he muttered as he applied the ice cubes wrapped in a cloth to her foot and held it there. 'Heaven only knows what we're going to do tomorrow if you can't stand on it.'

You could always get Bianca to do your cooking for you, Jessamy thought bitterly. After all, *she* was directly responsible for all this. But she held her tongue. Now she had the perfect opportunity to tell him about the cruel trick Bianca and Barry had played, nothing would have dragged it out of her. Pride, hurt, injured feelings, the sheer uselessness of trying to exonerate herself kept her silent, since both Bianca and Barry would deny their culpability in the plot and Luke had shown only too clearly what little trust he placed in her truthfulness.

She leaned back and closed her eyes so she didn't have to look at the dark head bowed before her and fight back the longing to run her fingers through the crisp hair. And she wondered how she *could* still love this man who had such a very low opinion of her. Anger at the injustice he had meted out in his readiness to think the worst of her should have destroyed all tender feelings she had for him.

She didn't see his eyes go to her white face as she sighed. 'It's going down,' he said gruffly. 'I'll get you some aspirin.'

He put the glass of water in her hand and while she swallowed the tablets he bound her ankle firmly with an elastic bandage to give support. 'Now don't you dare put that to the ground again till I say so,' he ordered, picking up the first aid box.

And how did he expect her to get to bed? she wondered angrily as the door closed behind him. Or was she supposed to sleep in this—she plucked at the soft silk folds of the kingfisher blue dress. It gave her a savage satisfaction to disobey him as she undressed and hobbled over to the washbasin to clean her teeth.

He woke her early next morning before the alarm went off. 'How's the ankle this morning?'

Jessamy waggled her foot under the duvet. 'Much better, thank you,' she said politely.

'Well, you hadn't better put any weight on it yet. I'll get the early morning tea and see to the breakfast.'

If he'd said it kindly she would have been grateful for his thoughtfulness, but his tone was so long-suffering she would be damned if she'd let him make a martyr of himself. Her ankle was much better, but it was far from recovered, as she discovered when she tried to walk on it. But provided she took things slowly and was careful not to put her full weight on it, she found she was mobile enough.

It took her some time to wash and dress and Luke was still busy with the teas as Jessamy cautiously opened her cabin door. She saw he was at the far end of the boat, just knocking on Bianca's door, so, confident he would be detained there for some time, she slipped out of her cabin and limped quietly down the gangway in her sneakers.

'What the hell do you think you're doing!' he exploded as he came into the galley and found her busy at the stove.

'Getting the breakfast, of course,' she retorted, trying not to quail at his forceful anger.

'I told you I'd do that.' He tried to take the pan from her, but she snatched it back.

'And have you chalk up another black mark against me for falling down on the job?' she flung at him bitterly. 'No, thank you, I can manage.'

He stood there fuming, looking for all the world as if he would like to strangle her with his bare hands. 'You really are the most exasperating, aggravating——'

It was like a knife being twisted in Jessamy's heart, because the last time he had said that he had finished, '. . . and utterly unforgettable . . .'

'I don't think you ought to finish that quotation,' she broke in, looking at him levelly, 'when we both know you don't mean it.'

A spasm seemed to cross his face and she knew he was remembering when he'd used those words before, and remembering too how he'd gone on. Now, with a muffled oath, he turned on his heel and stalked out.

But not many minutes later he was back and grabbing a stool, pushed her down on it, slipped off her canvas sneaker and began to unwrap the bandage. 'Minnie had this hidden away in one of her bags.' He shook an aerosol can. 'She swears by it for twists and sprains.' He aimed the can and pressed the button. It was like being sprayed with liquid ice, and Jessamy gasped in shock.

He glanced up at her. 'It hurts?'

She shook her head. 'Just cold. My foot feels numb.'

Luke nodded and strapped the bandage back on. 'Minnie says to leave this with you and every time the ankle starts to hurt, spray it again. And for heaven's sake try to rest it as much as possible.'

There had been a gentleness in his touch that had brought her old longing for him surging up again, and in self-defence she said bitterly, 'I know. You can't afford to have me laid up.'

'I didn't say that.'

'No, but it's what you meant.'

He stared at her for several moments, bafflement in his eyes, and some of the rock-hardness seemed to go out of his face, leaving him looking as unhappy as she felt herself. 'Jessamy——'

Her heart missed a beat and she didn't dare breathe. And then the moment was gone as Barry blundered into the galley. 'Breakfast ready yet, Jess?' Whatever Luke had been going to say remained unsaid. His jaws clamped together and he walked out.

Jessamy turned such a face of naked misery to Barry he couldn't meet her eyes, and he too walked out in the opposite direction.

At breakfast a number of the party expressed a wish to stay on long enough in Stratford to attend morning service at Holy Trinity Church, and though Luke didn't look any too pleased at having his schedule upset, he could hardly refuse their request. To make up for lost time he curtly suggested to Jessamy that she should provide the kind of lunch they could eat as they cruised instead of mooring for a cooked meal, so she spent her morning preparing salads and tasty open sandwiches, asparagus rolls and cucumber stuffed with cheese and herbs, most of which she was able to do sitting on her high stool to rest her foot.

But where she had once found pleasure and great satisfaction in her work, now her desperate loneliness and unhappiness made it a chore. As the guests returned from church and they were able to set off on the return journey, she longed for it to be over. She didn't think she could take much more of seeing Luke's stony, unforgiving face every day, knowing he believed her to be a wanton tease, deceitful and untrustworthy.

The canal was busier on this leg of the trip with the first week of June meaning the holiday season was well under way, and it began to take them longer to find a suitable secluded place to moor for the night. But when they reached Warwick they were able to see the castle perched on its crag beside the river Avon from their mooring. Jessamy had never visited it before and though she knew that besides being a repository of history and art treasures it was also one of the few medieval fortresses in England still habitable, she could raise no enthusiasm for seeing it now.

Barry had made several tentative overtures since they'd left Stratford, all of which Jessamy had cold-shouldered, but he came up behind her now as she gazed out of the window at what she could see of the ancient town.

'How about you and me going off on our own tomorrow, Jess?' he suggested. 'They'll all be too busy gawking at the sights to miss us.'

She slid out from beneath the hopeful arm around her shoulders. 'No, thank you. After I've done the necessary shopping I'm planning to spend the day resting in my cabin.'

'Aw, Jess——' He followed her up the galley, 'how long are you going to keep this up?'

She didn't answer. She was still too sickened by the way he'd ganged up with Bianca against her to be civil to him.

'Jess——' he persisted. 'Look, we're stuck with this job tootling up and down the canal, for the time being at least. Can't you forgive and forget? Things'll be better for us next trip, when Monro's not around.'

'If you really believe that, you're a bigger fool than I took you for,' Jessamy said wearily. 'Because for me there isn't going to be another trip. I've decided that being on the dole will be preferable to working for Luke under these conditions.'

Barry's face paled. 'But you can't throw your hand in, Jess. You promised! When Luke took over the marina you promised you'd stay too.'

'You really are incredible, Barry! You expect me to stand by you for the sake of friendship? And where was your friendship the other night? I'm sorry, but after that cruel trick you played I no longer feel I owe you any loyalty.' She pushed past him with a tray to set the tables in the dining saloon, hardening her heart against his shattered expression.

The towers of the castle rose out of a fine white mist the next morning when Jessamy got up, but the day promised to be hot once it cleared. She was pleased for the sake of the guests, but the prospect of blue skies only seemed to make the heavy stone she was carrying round with her in her chest even more painful.

She carried the first two trays back to *Hyacinth*, delivering Brad and Amy's first. It was as she was knocking on Minnie's door that she saw Barry emerge from Luke's cabin and walk past without a word. Not many minutes later she was surprised and relieved to see Luke leave the boat and walk quickly away towards the town. At least she wouldn't have the ordeal of having the tray snatched from her hand and the door slammed in her face again.

He was back by the time she was ready to serve breakfast, but although everyone else was making plans for what they intended to do with their day in Warwick, he didn't contribute to the conversation. Jessamy was just replenishing the coffee cups when there was a shrill cooee from the towpath, a thud as someone landed on the well deck and then the door was pushed open and a tall, angular girl said, 'Thank God it's the right boat! I was terrified I'd find myself walking into someone's bedroom.'

Bianca was the first to recover from her surprise. 'Nichola! What in the world are you doing here? I was just talking about you—telling Luke we ought to look you up while we're so near.'

'Come to take you off with me for the day, of course. I didn't think climbing around castles was *your* idea of fun,' the girl grinned.

'But how did you find us?' Bianca marvelled.

'Oh, Luke gave me a buzz,' the girl said casually, and Jessamy could have sworn she gave him a surreptitious wink, 'so I thought I'd come and collect you. Come on, then, are you ready? The car's only a hundred yards away. No, you won't need a coat. I'll bring her back safely, Luke, don't you worry, though it could be in the wee small hours. I've laid on a party in your honour tonight, Bianca—quite a few people you know and some you don't. It should be fun.'

Bianca was looking slightly bemused at this non-stop flow. 'But Luke's coming too. You are, aren't you, Luke?'

'I'm sorry, my pet, I only wish I could.' Luke lifted his shoulders helplessly. 'But I really can't abandon the rest of my guests for a whole day. You run along and enjoy yourself, though. I'll make out.'

'But——' Bianca looked torn between the delights her friend had to offer and her desire for Luke's company.

'Oh, do come on, Bianca, and stop twittering. I've invited people for sherry before lunch and I've heaps to show you first.' Nichola hustled Bianca off the boat before she could make any more protests.

There seemed to be a general lightening of spirits among the rest of the party at her departure, but some time later when Desmond, Minnie, Brad and Amy set off to explore the town, it appeared Luke had forgotten his assertion that he had to stay and entertain them, for he certainly didn't accompany them.

Jessamy had finished cleaning up the galley and was tidying and dusting the stateroom—not hurrying because the day stretched empty and lonely ahead—when Luke suddenly appeared in the doorway from the dining saloon. 'So this is where you're hiding! Sit down. You and I have got to talk,' he said curtly.

Jessamy stared at him in wide-eyed apprehension. Was he about to give her another scorching reprimand over another imagined misdemeanour? She tried to think of what she could possibly have done or left undone that had met with his displeasure. Clutching her duster and tense as a watch spring, she perched uneasily on the edge of a chair while he remained standing, towering over her, his face grim.

'Barry told me a very peculiar story this morning,' he said, his eyes fixed on her face. 'He says you were set up the other night, that you were tricked into his cabin and that I was *meant* to find you there.'

This was the last thing Jessamy had expected and she was so astounded she could only say, 'Barry told you? But why?'

'How the hell should I know why?' he said roughly. 'I only know he told me that was what happened. Is it true?'

Jessamy nodded, her heart thumping painfully. So that was why Barry had been to Luke's cabin this morning! But if Luke knew the truth about what had happened, why was he so angry with her still? 'I—I was on my way to bed when Bianca told me Barry was ill,' she faltered. 'I assume she went running straight to you, because your timing couldn't have been better. Barry was lying on the bed when I got to his cabin. I'd just put my hand on his head to see if he was running a temperature when he grabbed me. I was actually fighting him off when you walked in.'

She looked up nervously, but as he was silhouetted against the bright sunlight pouring in through the open door to the well deck, she was unable to see his expression.

'So I jumped to the wrong conclusion,' he said harshly. 'What I can't understand is why you made no attempt to explain! How the hell was I expected to know it wasn't what it looked like?'

Jessamy had a feeling of unreality. She couldn't imagine what had prompted Barry to own up, but now Luke knew the truth everything should have come right between them. Only it hadn't. For some reason he still seemed to be blaming her, and her own temper rose at this further injustice.

'And if I *had* tried to tell you what really happened——' she flung at him, 'you wouldn't have believed a word of it. Come on, admit it. You were only too ready to think the worst of me and you'd only have thought it was another pack of lies to get myself out of trouble. Oh yes, Bianca was very clever.'

'Bianca?' he stiffened. 'It was Barry's idea, because he was jealous of the attention I was paying you when he wanted you himself.'

Jessamy got up and walked to the doorway, still clutching her duster to stop her hands shaking. 'You see what I mean?' she threw over her shoulder. 'Even now you'll only believe what you want to believe.'

'What I *want* to believe?' he echoed angrily. 'Jessamy, don't you have the slightest idea how I felt, finding you there in Barry's bed? After I'd seen you very matey together earlier in the day too? I didn't *want* to believe what I saw, but how could I not, when you didn't have one word of excuse to offer?'

'I've already told you,' she said wearily, 'I knew you wouldn't believe me.' She turned to face him. 'I'm beginning to wonder if you really believe it now, in spite of Barry's confession.'

'What do you mean?' he rapped.

'That you're probably suspecting all this is a story cooked up by me and Barry to get me off the hook.'

In a stride Luke was grasping her shoulders fiercely. 'Is it?'

She didn't flinch. 'No, it isn't. And while we're flinging recriminations about—*I* find it difficult to understand how you could really think I would have gone voluntarily to Barry's bed when you know very well I've spent the last few weeks trying to put him off the idea of wanting to marry me.'

His fingers dug painfully into her shoulders as he shook her. 'You little fool! It was *because* I knew how much he wanted you. And it suddenly looked as if you wanted him after all. I thought you'd been lying to me, and that hurt.'

'And don't you think *I* was hurt too?' Tears stung her eyes and rose in a hard, painful lump in her throat. 'The way you looked at me. The cruel things you said. You treated me like a—like a leper.'

His grip relaxed and he groaned. 'Do you think I'm not remembering all that? Jessamy, I'm sorry—I'm sorry.' He drew her to him, his arms enfolding her, rocking her gently to and fro as if comforting a hurt child. His sudden tenderness after his bitter, accusing anger was too much for her and she sobbed weakly against his chest while he murmured endearments.

'Come on, dry your eyes,' he said when her storm of weeping had subsided. Taking out his handkerchief, he gently mopped her face. 'You're quite right, I suppose. I *would* have found it hard to believe if you'd tried to explain. But don't think too badly of me, Jessamy. It was such a damnable plot. How could I have suspected?'

His face was a blur as she looked up at him through tear-drenched eyes and traced the outline of his mouth with light fingers, a mouth that was no longer tight and unforgiving. She gave a little sigh because the memory of that granite hardness had left a scar.

He caught her hand, pressing it to his lips, kissing the fingers, the palm, until she trembled. 'I should have known my strait-laced little Jessamy couldn't be the girl she appeared to be,' he said thickly. 'I should have trusted you. When I think of the precious time we've wasted——'

# CHAPTER TEN

'ARE you going to try to find the others?' Jessamy asked. She was still breathless from Luke's abrupt change of mood, from anger to tenderness and then to exuberance, as he hurried her away from the boat and into the town.

'Not on your life!' Luke said at once. 'Now I've got you to myself for once, you don't think I'm voluntarily going to share you?'

Her heartbeats quickened at the possessive note in his voice but she still couldn't be sure exactly where she stood with him.

'What'll it be first?' he asked. 'The town or the castle?'

His exuberant mood was catching. 'Oh, the castle.' It had held no interest when the only prospect of seeing it was by herself, but now—'I was never any good at saving the best bits till last. Too greedy, I suppose.'

'You? Greedy?' He squeezed the hand he was holding. 'You don't know the meaning of the word!'

Oh, but she was greedy for some things, Jessamy thought. Luke's company—his love.

They paid their fee and passed through the impressive gatehouse, staring in awe at the thickness of the curtain wall with its massive tower defences that had remained intact for six hundred years. They had to join a guided tour when they would rather have wandered at will, but it made little difference to Jessamy, isolated as she was in her little bubble of happiness.

'You would have made a good baron,' she teased as they wandered through the Great Hall, its stone walls hung with ancient armour. 'I can just see you, robed in splendour, sitting in judgment on your vassals.'

'A gentle, mild-mannered man like me?' Luke protested.

She gave a slight shiver. 'You can be terrifying when you're angry.'

'Don't——' he said quickly, holding her close.

Then as they looked out of the windows at the sheer drop down to the river Avon below, Luke said, 'Well, if you can see me as the wicked baron, I can see you as the gentle lady Jessamy, wringing your hands and mopping your tears with your golden hair, waiting for your wicked baron to come home from the wars.' The expression in his eyes as he looked at her made the breath catch in her throat.

They wandered on at the tail of the guided tour through room after room, not listening to the information that was offered but preferring to use their imagination to make up their own stories about the people who had lived in the castle through the centuries.

Strolling later through the grounds was even more magical, for here there was no one to hurry them on when they wanted to linger to watch a peacock spread its magnificent tail, or to frown at their hilarity when they imagined what a party they could have if the celebrated Warwick Vase, that was reputed to hold one hundred and sixty one gallons, was filled with champagne.

But magical as it all was as they bought a picnic lunch of crusty rolls and Stilton cheese and ate it lolling on the grass beside the Avon, Jessamy couldn't quite dispel her reservations. She hadn't been joking when she told Luke she had found his anger terrifying. She could understand his reason for being angry. He had made no secret of the fact that he found her desirable, so it must have been a painful blow to his pride when he had discovered—as he thought—that she had succumbed to Barry when she had steadfastly denied Luke the same favours. What still disturbed her was the fact that his anger, and the cruel streak that anger had revealed, had had such a devastating effect on her, hurting her so terribly. She recognised now the reason for her instinctive fear of him right from the beginning. It was fear of the power he had to hurt her.

She let her eyes wander over the long, powerful body stretched out at ease on the grass beside her and the desire his nearness always provoked stirred in her. She shivered as if a cloud had just covered the sun, though the sky was clear. She couldn't help loving him, but she didn't trust him any more than she had in the beginning. He had already shown how unscrupulous he was, deliberately putting Barry out of business in order to take over the marina himself. How could she be sure he wasn't equally unscrupulous in love, especially as the word hadn't appeared in his vocabulary? He'd never pretended he loved her, he only wanted her. And if she gave in to his demands—what then?

Her mouth went dry with excitement and her limbs felt heavy as she imagined what it might be like, surrendering to him completely, and a traitorous little voice in her head prompted, 'Why not? Would it be so very dreadful to snatch at what happiness was offered?' She shivered again, knowing instinctively that if she gave herself to Luke, it would be irrevocable. She would never be able to watch him walk out of her life once his desire for her had burned itself out, as it inevitably would. She wasn't naïve enough to imagine there was anything permanent in his feelings for her. There was Bianca, for one thing. Minnie Asher had said Bianca meant to marry Luke. Maybe that was just Minnie's gossip, but whatever their relationship, Bianca obviously played a large part in Luke's life. She only had to remember his refusal to believe the girl was in any way to blame for setting Jessamy up in that compromising situation with Barry.

And yet sometimes when she saw the tender expression in Luke's eyes she could almost believe it wasn't all lust, that he really did care about her just a little. She sighed, unhappy and confused.

'I hope that was a sigh of contentment.' Luke rolled over and lifted himself on one elbow, looking down into her face. 'You've been very quiet. What were you thinking about?'

A flush crept up her cheeks and she sat up to tidy the remains of their picnic, for she could never tell him of the doubts and fears that crowded her mind. 'I was just wondering if the others are enjoying their day,' she prevaricated. 'Wasn't it strange, that friend of Bianca's turning up out of the blue this morning?'

'Nothing strange about it at all, since I arranged it.' Luke grinned and as she stared at him open-mouthed she remembered Nichola's surreptitious wink. 'After Barry made his confession this morning I knew you and I had to have a serious talk, and that would have been impossible with Bianca around. So I went off to find a phone and arrange for Nichola to take her off my hands.'

He sounded pleased with himself for the way he had manipulated everything to his satisfaction, and maybe she should feel flattered that he had chosen to spend the day with her rather than Bianca, but she couldn't help wondering if one day he would be arranging for someone to take herself off his hands.

But she refused to think about that just now. She still had today and she meant to make the most of it. It might be all she would have. 'Come on, lazybones, you promised to show me the town.' She sprang up and pulled him to his feet.

They wandered hand in hand up one street and down another, gazing into shop windows, venturing into side alleys, climbing to the chapel of St James, an incredible eight hundred and fifty years old, built over the West gate of the town beside the timber framed Lord Leycester's hospital erected by Robert Dudley, Queen Elizabeth the First's favourite, to house twelve 'poor and impotent' people of the town. And for Jessamy there was only the ancient past and the here and now, because she couldn't let herself admit to a future that might not hold Luke.

'Oh, it's been a lovely day!' Jessamy breathed when they were retracing their steps to the hotel-boats.

He kissed her quickly right there on the towpath. 'Bianca's going to a party tonight, so why don't we have one of our own? Go and rest that ankle for an hour, then put on your warpaint. Wear that bronze dress, the one that looks as if you've been poured into it.' He gave her a little push towards *Hyacinth's* gangway. 'Though don't hold me responsible for my actions if you do!'

It was quite a party. A 'proper knees up', as Minnie called it, for everyone entered into the party spirit. Acting on Luke's instructions Barry popped the champagne corks and kept everyone's glass filled, and when Luke insisted Jessamy was still off duty, it was Desmond Britton and Minnie who raided her cold store and laid on supper.

Luke provided the right kind of music on his tape deck and they all danced, even Minnie—especially Minnie, who gave them a very lively demonstration of the traditional cockney dance, the Lambeth Walk, skipping nimbly on her shapely legs and not seeming to notice her bulk, while they all sang the tune. Luke and Jessamy were trying it out for themselves when they were suddenly aware of Bianca standing in the doorway staring, taking in the champagne glasses, the debris of the supper, the laughing, happy faces.

'What *is* going on?' she demanded peevishly as the

singers fell silent. 'I thought everyone would be in bed hours ago.'

'I suppose it is late.' Luke looked down at Jessamy still leaning breathless against him and his arm tightened round her shoulders. 'We were having such fun we didn't notice the time.'

'So I see.' Bianca's voice was crusted with ice and her bottom lip drooped. 'You didn't tell me *you* would be having a party.'

'Oh, it was just a spur-of-the-moment thing,' Luke assured her. 'I'm sure you've had a much more interesting time at Nichola's do.'

'As a matter of fact it was super.' Bianca tossed her head. 'And a very charming man brought me back.'

If she hoped that would make Luke jealous she was disappointed. 'Good for you, darling,' he said heartily. 'And now we should all go to bed.'

Jessamy automatically began to clear up, but Luke caught her hand. 'Not tonight,' he said softly, his eyes caressing her.

Bianca's mouth tightened and her eyes sharpened in suspicion. With a last reassuring squeeze of Jessamy's hand he said cheerfully, 'Come on, Bianca. I'll walk you back to your cabin and you can tell me about the fleshpots you've been dipping in tonight.'

Bianca twined a possessive arm around his waist, but there was still hostility and suspicion in the glance she darted at Jessamy.

The next morning found Jessamy humming softly to herself as she worked, as if some of the previous day's magic still clung to her. 'You sound happy,' Barry called through the open galley door from the rear deck where he stood at the tiller.

Jessamy took the basin she was stirring outside. 'Barry, thanks for coming clean with Luke and telling him what really happened that night.'

He reddened but said nothing.

'Why *did* you tell him?' she asked softly. 'It couldn't have been easy.'

His eyes flicked to her and away again. 'Because I couldn't stand having you hate me so much.'

She was deeply touched. The trick he had played on her was cruel, but by having the courage to confess he had more than earned her forgiveness. 'I don't hate you any more.' She kissed his cheek. 'Thanks.'

'You don't have to thank me,' he muttered, reddening even more. 'But you will change your mind about throwing your hand in, won't you, Jess? You needn't be afraid of me bothering you any more, I know I can't possibly compete with what Monro's got to offer, but I couldn't stick this job without having you along.'

Jessamy agreed she would say no more about leaving, but she felt horribly guilty again as she realised how painful it must be for Barry, having to watch her making a fool of herself over the man who had cheated him out of his business. It was shaming to be so besottedly in love with Luke that it didn't seem to matter he was unscrupulous and ruthlessly selfish, shaming to hide her hurt while he danced attendance on Bianca and to be so grateful for the few sweet minutes he could spare for her.

Her tension mounted as they drew nearer to the long tunnel that had had such a claustrophobic effect on her on the outward journey. She was in the galley, and although she had known all along she had this ordeal to face again and had told herself firmly she wasn't going to make such a fuss this time, against all reason her panic began to rise. But within moments of Barry's warning call, Luke was there beside her.

He took one look at her frightened face. 'Darling, you're going to be all right. Come and sit down. The light's on and I'll stay with you.'

'N-not the stateroom,' she gasped. 'They'll all stare——'

'No, the dining saloon. We'll be alone there.' Helping her with one arm firmly round her waist, he sat on one of the benches and pulled her close.

She was looking fearfully out of the window and when the sunshine was abruptly cut off and the light from the window shone on dank walls, she began to shake. Luke took his arms away for a moment to swish the curtains across, and she made an instinctive movement towards him. But then he was holding her again and she felt safe. 'It's all right,' he soothed. 'I won't let you go.'

'Luke!'

He raised his head sharply at the scandalised voice from the doorway. 'Bianca, would you please go away,' he said coldly. 'Can't you see Jessamy's ill?'

'And you're kissing her better, I suppose,' she retorted with outraged sarcasm, ignoring his request. 'There might be some excuse to fall for the claustrophobia trick once, but to be taken in by it again——'

'My God, Bianca, but you're a heartless little bitch!' His voice was like a whiplash, and the girl's mouth fell open in astonishment.

'Luke! If you're going to talk to me like that I shall wish I'd never come on this trip.'

'And I'm beginning to wish I'd never asked you,' he said savagely. 'Now are you going or do you want me to put you out?'

Bianca gasped. 'All right. *Let* her make a fool of you!' She slammed the door behind her with a resounding crash.

Jessamy felt the tension leave him. 'Oh dear,' he said ruefully. 'I should never have said that—about wishing I'd never asked her.'

'Why n-not—if it— it's true?' She was still having difficulty with her panic breathing in spite of the suddenly flaring quarrel taking her mind off the appalling feeling of being buried alive.

'She'll only make me suffer for it later. But I dare say I'll cope, so let's forget about her. We must be nearly through now. You're doing very well. Just relax.' Between each word he kissed her mouth, very quickly and very gently, like little sips from a honeypot, and with each kiss stirring her blood, the panic subsided. She began to breathe normally again.

'There, it wasn't so bad, was it?' he said gently.

Jessamy gave a shaky smile and shook her head. It was difficult to equate this gentle, tender Luke with the hard, ruthless, unprincipled man she knew him to be. 'I wish you were always like this,' she said impulsively. He raised an interrogative eyebrow and she rushed on, 'Well, you're two men, aren't you? I mean there's this side of you, so gentle and—and caring. But then there's the businessman.' A cloud passed over her face. 'The man who——'

'—Cheated Barry out of the marina?' he finished for her. 'Oh, I haven't forgotten that particular accusation.' He held her at arms' length so she had a clear view of his face. 'I did *not* cheat Barry out of his business, Jessamy. I don't operate that way, and anyway I didn't need to. Perhaps he neglected to tell you the bank had already refused to extend his overdraft and were demanding the outstanding debt be paid off? So even if I *had* renewed his lease, he would have been out of business in days. As it is, Barry now has money in the bank and a steady job instead of crushing debts he had no chance of paying off.'

It had the ring of truth. Jessamy felt as if a great weight had been taken from her heart.

'So you see——' a wry smile curved Luke's mouth, 'I'm not quite the rogue you believe me.'

'I—I'm sorry.' She coloured in embarrassed shame when she recalled some of the names she'd once called him to his face. 'I really am sorry. I didn't have any right to judge you.'

'Just as I didn't have any right to judge you at Stratford. Shall we call it quits and begin again?' He didn't wait for her answer before claiming her all too eager mouth.

There was a sound by the door and his head jerked up. 'I thought I said—oh, it's you, Minnie.'

'Don't mind me, ducks,' the little cockney woman said cheerfully. 'I only come to see as Jess's okay, an' I can see she is.' She chuckled. 'An' if you want to pretend we're still in that tunnel, s'all right by me!'

Luke flicked open the curtains and the sunlight poured in. They looked at each other and started to laugh.

But Jessamy was far from laughing later on that evening. She had hurried over to *Hyacinth* to shower and change before serving up the dinner, and as this would be the last night on the boat she decided to put the clothes she had just taken off straight into her suitcase. Lifting it down from the top of the wardrobe, she heard something rattle inside. It was a small leather box. Puzzled, she undid the catch and a pair of diamond ear-rings winked up at her.

They were very distinctive ear-rings, each small diamond set on the end of a stalk so fine it trembled when the wearer moved, and Jessamy recognised them at once. Bianca had worn them at the theatre in Stratford!

Her mind whirled. There was only one way they could have got into her suitcase and that was for Bianca to have put them there herself. But why? Certainly not as a gift! Gooseflesh prickled her skin. If such a valuable item of jewellery had been planted on her deliberately, Bianca must be intending to accuse her of stealing them!

Sick anger churned her up at this new attempt of Bianca's to discredit her, but slowly it gave way to a feeling of triumph. Surely Luke would *have* to believe

her this time. Here was the evidence in her hand. If she
took the ear-rings to him and told him where she'd
found them——

The feeling of triumph shrivelled. Bianca could still
twist it against her, if she accused Jessamy of taking the
ear-rings only to bring this accusation. The girl could
look so innocent and sound so convincing, and Luke
had already shown that in his eyes she could do no
wrong. Who would Luke believe? 'Trust me,' he'd said,
and she wanted to so much, but she knew she didn't
dare put it to the test.

She snapped the lid of the box shut on the hateful
things. If she couldn't take this problem to Luke, she
had at least to protect herself. Hurrying down the silent
boat, she opened the door of Bianca's untidy cabin. The
dressing table was littered with perfume bottles,
cosmetics and a white silk scarf left in a crumpled heap.
She put the small box down among the litter and let the
scarf drop over it.

Jessamy was clearing away the dessert plates and as
Luke rose to lead the party back to the stateroom for
their coffee, Bianca put a restraining hand on his arm.
'Luke darling, I didn't want to spoil everyone's dinner,
but I must tell you something very disturbing has
happened. My diamond ear-rings—you know, the ones
you gave me for my birthday? They've disappeared
from my cabin!'

Jessamy had been very tense as she'd served dinner,
waiting for this moment, but now all she felt was a
painful pang at learning the ear-rings had been a
present from Luke.

'Don't be silly, Bianca. They couldn't have disappeared. You must have mislaid them.' Luke stood up
again. 'I'll help you find them when we've had our
coffee.'

'Well, naturally that's what I thought too,' Bianca
said quickly. 'But I've already looked, Luke. I've

searched everywhere and they're just not there. Even the box has gone, the brown leather one I kept them in.'

'Well, if you haven't mislaid them, would you mind telling me where you think they *could* have disappeared to?' Luke said irritably.

'Somebody must have taken them, of course.' Bianca let her temper show at his obtuseness.

Luke's face was suddenly rigid. 'Be careful, Bianca. You can't seriously be accusing someone here of being a thief.'

'Really, Bianca, that's an outrageous accusation to make!' Amy Francis bridled. 'You surely don't think *I* had anything to do with it?'

'More like it's *me* she's pointin' the finger at,' Minnie said tartly. 'I mean, you c'n just see *me* wearin' diamond ear-rings, can't you?'

Two spots of colour burned in Bianca's cheeks, but she said doggedly, 'All I'm saying is that the ear-rings have disappeared. And we all know there's *one* person with free access to all our cabins.' She looked straight at Jessamy.

'Bianca, I'll not have this.' Luke's eyes were blazing. 'You'll take that back and apologise to Jessamy at once!'

'I'll do no such thing!' Bianca quivered with temper.

'I don't think an apology would be enough.' Even though she had been ready for it Jessamy still felt sick that the other girl had carried through her plan. 'Bianca has accused me of stealing and until those ear-rings are found the mud's going to stick. I don't have anything to be afraid of, so go ahead and search my cabin.'

'No!' Luke objected violently. 'The whole idea's preposterous!'

He was so vehement Jessamy wondered if she should have trusted him after all, but it was too late now. 'I think I should at least be given the chance to clear my name,' she said quietly, and saw the little smile of satisfaction curve Bianca's lips.

Jessamy led the way to *Hyacinth*, opening her cabin door and standing back for Luke and Bianca to enter.

'Well, Bianca?' Luke stood waiting. 'Jessamy has given you permission to invade her privacy.'

'But I thought you——' She bit her lip. Jessamy saw her eyes flick to the suitcase on top of the wardrobe, but Bianca didn't make the mistake of going straight to it. She opened a drawer in the dressing table and rummaged perfunctorily before moving on to the next.

Jessamy opened the wardrobe door herself. 'Don't forget to look in the toes of my shoes, and of course my jacket pockets.'

Bianca coloured faintly at her contempt but continued the charade of leaving no stone unturned. And when a search of the lockers beneath the bed revealed nothing she pretended to notice for the first time the suitcase on the wardrobe. 'There,' she said, pointing. 'She'll be leaving the boat tomorrow. That's the likeliest place.' Silently Luke reached it down for her. She flung back the lid and stared into the empty interior in disbelief.

'Now, if we might do what *I* wanted to do in the first place—search your own cabin, Bianca——' Luke said tightly.

He stopped on the threshold, regarding the untidy cabin with distaste. 'How you ever find anything in here . . . Where do you keep your jewellery?'

Sulkily Bianca snatched open a drawer and took out a leather case which she thumped down on the dressing table, scattering several bottles. Searching for the key among the litter, she moved the silk scarf. Luke pounced. 'And what do you call this?' he snapped open the brown box and the diamonds glittered.

'They weren't there earlier, I swear they weren't.' Bianca ran her tongue over her lips as if they'd suddenly gone dry.

Luke didn't even bother to argue. 'Don't ever make such an unfounded accusation again, Bianca.'

'It—it was a mistake. I'm sorry,' she muttered.

'I suppose that's all the apology you'll get.' His angry eyes softened as he turned to Jessamy and took her arm. 'Let's get out of here.'

'Wait! I—I'd like Jessamy to stay if she will so I can apologise to her properly.'

Luke nodded grimly. 'I'm glad you realise you owe her that.'

But no apology was forthcoming when the door had closed behind Luke. 'You're like a cat with nine lives,' Bianca hissed. 'I suppose you found them and went through that charade to make me look foolish!'

'You meant me to look a lot worse than foolish,' Jessamy retorted. 'You would have branded me a thief.'

'And no more than you deserve, the way you've poached shamelessly on my preserves!'

'*Your* preserves——' Jessamy began hotly, but Bianca wouldn't let her finish.

'*My* preserves,' she insisted. 'Didn't Luke mention it? No, it's hardly a subject he'd want to bring up with a girl he was trying to lay. As soon as we get back to London we're announcing our engagement.'

Jessamy felt the colour drain from her face. 'I don't believe you,' she whispered.

'Oh, come on——' Bianca jeered. 'Wishful thinking can't have made you *that* blind. All right, so Barry let me down and got you out of one corner I'd backed you into, but why else did Luke let the matter drop, even though he knew I was responsible? And why, if you're so sure it's you Luke loves, didn't you take the ear-rings to him when you found them?' she added softly.

'I—I——' But Jessamy had no answer. Unerringly Bianca had probed the aching centre of all her doubts and fears.

# CHAPTER ELEVEN

THEY were on the home stretch. Very soon now they would be dropping down the flight of locks to the marina. Purple thunderclouds were massing on the horizon and it was very hot, that sticky, airless heat that made Jessamy's head pound after her sleepless night.

'Bianca doesn't own me,' Luke had said to her once. 'Trust me.' And she really had begun to trust him, but Bianca had been terribly convincing. Would she have lied about their engagement when, if it *was* a lie, time would soon prove it? And if there was this understanding between Bianca and Luke it would explain so much—his kid-glove handling of her, his unwillingness to hear anything against her. Round and round her thoughts went, trapped in a treadmill, her heart wanting to believe Bianca was lying but her head all too fearful that she was not. Her shirt clung stickily to her back as she dumped the rubbish out on the rear deck.

'Hope we make it before the storm breaks.' Barry looked happy and excited. 'It's great getting back. I say, Jess, did Luke tell you——'

'Miss Daunay——' Desmond Britton called to her from the galley and she had to go inside before Barry could finish, 'Ah, Miss Daunay—Jessamy, I couldn't leave without congratulating you on the high standard you've kept up these last two weeks.' There was the nearest thing to enthusiasm she had yet seen on his face.

'Why, thank you, Mr Britton.' So much had happened on this trip she had almost forgotten the importance of pleasing this man. 'Does that mean you're going to give us a glowing write-up?'

'I shall certainly give the enterprise a column or

two——' He gave her a dry, wintry smile, '——though I would be able to write with more conviction if *you* had been continuing as hostess. Such a pity Luke thinks you're unsuitable.'

Jessamy's own smile wavered as she tried not to betray her shock.

'I tried to talk to him.' Desmond went on. 'Only last night I told him it wasn't in his best interests to let you go, but he said he already had a well recommended married couple to take over. And I suppose you have other plans. Whatever they are, my dear, I wish you luck.' Nodding affably, he wandered off, leaving Jessamy in a state of shock.

Of course Luke had talked of her work—and Barry's—on the hotel-boats as only temporary, just to set up the operation, but—— 'Unsuitable!' The word rankled. Luke would *have* to explain it.

But she found everyone, Luke among them, his arm lightly round Bianca's shoulders, crowded out on the well deck watching the ruined lock-keeper's cottage appear round the bend. Now was not the time to tackle him.

She went back to the galley and Brad Francis followed her. 'Jessamy my dear, thank you for making this a wonderful trip.' He took her hand in his hot, podgy one and held on to it. 'My only regret is that I didn't get the chance to know you better.' He moved in closer, pinning her against the cupboards. 'But there's going to be time for that when we're working together.'

'Working together?' Jessamy stared at the red, sweating face only inches from her own. 'I don't understand you.'

'Why, when I'm managing the marina, of course.' He leered at her. 'Didn't Luke tell you I was going to be your new boss?'

Her flesh crawling, Jessamy pushed him away, and the lurch as the boat bumped the bank and stopped

helped. It couldn't be true! Barry was going to manage
the marina. Luke couldn't go back on his word. But
that offer had been made before Barry had joined forces
with Bianca to play that nasty trick. Even so, Luke
couldn't be so unfair as to sack Barry while Bianca went
scot free! More than that—he was going to marry Bianca!

'Jess—the locks,' Barry called from the rear deck.
'Give Luke a hand or we'll be here all day.'

Shaking with anger, Jessamy sprang from the rear
deck on to the bank. Luke was already halfway to the
first lock gate, carrying the windlass. She ran after him.
'How *could* you!' she burst out. 'I wouldn't have
believed anyone could be so callous and underhand!'

He stared at her in surprise. 'How could I what? And
whatever it is, can't it wait till we've got rid of all these
people?'

'No, it can't.' She planted herself firmly in his path.
'Sacking Barry, I mean. All right, what he did was
wrong, but at least he had the guts to own up, which is
more than Bianca did.'

'Now look here——' His brows drew together and
there was an edge to his voice that was echoed in the
first rumble of thunder.

Jessamy didn't want to hear him defending Bianca
again. 'Brad Francis was lying, then, when he said
you'd made *him* manager of the marina?'

His frown deepened. 'No, but——'

'And you won't deny you told Desmond Britton
you're replacing me on the hotel-boat?'

'No, I won't deny it, but Jessamy—please——' He
tried to take her arm but she threw him off.

'Don't touch me! I'm sick of you manipulating
people as if they were toy soldiers. And I was almost
fool enough to believe I'd misjudged you! Well,
Bianca's welcome to you. You're a devious pair and
should be well suited. Just don't expect a telegram of
congratulation from *me* on your engagement!'

Choking, she turned and ran down the path towards the marina.

'Jessamy——'

She ignored his call, the hurt inside her almost tearing her apart, blind instinct urging her to put as much space between herself and the source of that hurt as possible. Blind instinct too drove her to make for the shortest distance to the haven of her houseboat on the lagoon.

Hundreds of times before she had crossed the narrow, single-railed footbridge over the lock, but never before in quite such an emotional turmoil or with her eyes blinded by tears. She was halfway across when the jagged fork of lightning split the sky with an almost instantaneous crack of thunder. Startled, she slipped, and then she was falling, falling interminably it seemed down the narrow, deep lock, until she hit the green water at the bottom and it closed over her head.

She rose to the surface, gasping and choking. Reaching out, she tried to get a finger-hold on the wall to hold herself above the water, but the wall was wet and slippery and she only succeeded in pushing herself under again. She had learned to swim as a child, but never hampered with wet clothes, and it felt as if a giant hand was dragging her down. Her lungs were bursting, the water seemed to explode and boil around her.

And then instead of dragging her down, something was pushing her up again. Her head broke the surface. She choked for air and blinked as Luke's head bobbed up beside her. 'For pity's sake stop fighting me, you little fool! Relax, just relax, and I can hold you up.'

She spluttered, coughing up water, and at last got some air into her lungs. Luke's hand slipped on the slimy wall and his head disappeared. She thrashed around in panic and there was a stinging pain in her cheek as he slapped her. 'Please—keep calm. I don't want to have to knock you out.' His head was beside her again, his strong arms supporting her. With a supreme effort she let herself go limp.

Luke managed to dig his fingers into a crevice and this time he held on. But the green, slimy walls rose sheer, ten—twelve feet above their heads. It was like being at the bottom of a well. They were never going to climb up there. Panic stiffened her limbs again and made her breathing shallow and jerky. The walls were leaning in on her, burying her alive—The terror was too much, and merciful blackness closed over her.

The light was pressing against her eyelids, but she didn't want to wake up. She had been having such a lovely dream—Luke holding her close, begging her not to leave him, telling her he loved her——

There was a heavy tread beside her bed. Her eyes flew open and she found herself gazing at the familiar patch of ceiling over her own bed on her houseboat.

'So you've decided to wake up at last, 'ave you?'

'Minnie! What are you doing here?'

'Lookin' after you, of course,' the little cockney woman retorted. 'An' I 'ope I never go through another panic like that. Thought you was a goner when they dragged you out o' that lock!'

Memory came rushing back and Jessamy struggled to sit up. Brought *her* out! What about—— 'Luke!' she demanded, a terrible fear clutching at her. 'Is he all right? He wasn't——'

''E's all right, ducks.' Minnie pushed her back against the pillows. 'Proper wore out, but it'd take more'n a drop o' water to finish 'im.'

Jessamy subsided dispiritedly. Of course, he would have gone back to London with Bianca for their engagement party.

'Sat up with you all night, 'e did, an' I only got 'im to take a bit o' rest when I promised as I'd wake him when you come to.'

Jessamy sat up again. 'You mean he's still here? He didn't go back to London with Bianca?'

'While you was still more dead than alive? I should just think 'e didn't! Nearly demented, 'e's been, even though the doctor said you was only shocked and gave you somethin' to knock you out.'

Jessamy shook her head in confusion. 'You said he sat up with me all *night*?' It had been late Saturday morning when she fell into the lock. 'What time is it now?'

Minnie looked at her watch. 'Six o'clock of a Sunday mornin'. 'Ere, where do you think you're goin'?' Jessamy had swung her legs out of bed and was standing shakily.

'I'm all right, really I am,' Jessamy reassured her quickly. 'At least I shall be if you'll only let me get to the loo!' Minnie's laughter followed her down the passageway.

She was returning to her room when the door of the spare cabin opened. Luke's hair was rumpled, his face grey under the dark stubble, and it was all too obvious he had slept in his clothes. 'You look awful,' she said.

'You're not exactly a vision of loveliness yourself,' he retorted, then with a groan he gathered her fiercely into his arms. 'Oh, my love—I thought I'd lost you——'

''Ere, that's enough o' that! You bring 'er back to bed this minute,' Minnie ordered.

Luke obeyed at once, picking Jessamy up and laying her tenderly back on her bed. 'All right, Minnie, but you must let us talk for a few minutes. There are one or two things we have to get sorted out.'

'Just as long as it takes to make a cuppa tea, then.' Minnie closed the door carefully behind her.

'Now then——' he sat in the bed beside her, 'who was the one to jump to the wrong conclusion *this* time? If you'd given me the chance to explain you might not have thought it necessary to throw yourself into the lock.'

'I didn't,' she said indignantly. 'I slipped. And I don't know about wrong conclusions. You admitted——'

'Let's take them one by one, shall we?' he broke in. 'First, yes, I have given Brad Francis the job of managing the marina. I know he's a randy old devil, but he'll be good at the job. And I have *not* sacked Barry. Negotiations are nearly complete for taking over the boat repair yard in Market Swinford. The idea is to move all the marina repair work there and let Barry run the whole shot. He seemed delighted at the prospect.'

'Oh.' She was remembering Barry trying to tell her something only minutes before the accident, but she hadn't had time to listen. No wonder he'd been so excited, if this was his news. It was a job far better suited to him than managing the marina.

'Two——' Luke went on inexorably, 'of course I'm taking you off the hotel-boats. You don't think I'd subject you to the torture of going through that tunnel every week, do you? Besides, I don't see any future in having my wife living apart from me all summer.'

'Your wife!' Jessamy's eyes widened in shock. 'But you don't——'

'There you go again, telling me what I don't want. Haven't I got it through that stubborn skull of yours yet that I love you?' His voice softened. 'I want you to marry me, darling, and even if you say no I'll keep on asking, because I just can't imagine living without you now.'

Jessamy's heart was thumping so hard she could barely breathe. Surely she had to be dreaming again? 'But Bianca—your engagement—She said you'd be announcing it as soon as you got back to London.'

'And you believed her?' Luke's dark eyebrows arched.

'I didn't want to, but——' She twisted her hands

together. 'I didn't see how she'd dare make such a claim if it wasn't true, and it all added up—your refusal to think badly of her however outrageously she behaved.'

There was a strange look on Luke's face, almost triumphant. 'So that was the real reason you ran off and tumbled into the lock!' He gathered her up in his arms and hugged her jubilantly. 'Now I know you love me. Oh, darling, we're going to be so happy!'

It was very pleasant there in his arms, but she still didn't understand. 'Luke——'

'Darling, let me explain about Bianca.' He settled himself against her pillows, holding her tightly. 'She's a spoilt brat, and believe me, I have no illusions about her character—I've known her far too long. But I do feel kind of responsible for her. You see, her father, an old friend, was a great deal of help to me when I was a boy and when I first started out in business. He was a financier, very wealthy and powerful, until he started to make mistakes. His empire crashed six months ago and he shot himself rather than face bankruptcy. So poor Bianca, born with a golden spoon in her mouth and brought up to do nothing but spend money, suddenly didn't have a bean and had lost the father she adored too.

'I tried to help—got her some modelling work. She was good at it—when she remembered to turn up for appointments. Then a couple of months ago I thought she was going to be taken off my hands when the Honourable Justin Pope was burning to marry her. Only her tantrums cooled his passion rather fast and he took off for America. That's why I asked her on the trip, to try to cheer her up. Unfortunately, as Justin had escaped her, she seemed to have made up her mind I'd make a good substitute.'

So far from being the ruthless knave she had thought him, manipulating everyone to his own selfish ends, he was in fact a warmhearted and compassionate man.

Perhaps she would have saved them both a lot of pain if only she had trusted the instinct of her heart.

'Bianca was never in love with you, then?' Jessamy couldn't imagine any girl knowing Luke and not loving him.

'I doubt if she's capable of loving anyone but herself,' he said wryly. 'And I've certainly never been in love with her. In fact I know now I've never really loved anyone until I met you. Nobody's ever made me as angry as you, or made me laugh so much.' His arms tightened and his voice was husky. 'Or made me as afraid as I was when I saw you fall into that lock.'

Jessamy was remembering that awful moment after she had woken this morning and had feared *he* hadn't got out alive, and in a convulsive movement she twisted round and clung to him. His mouth claimed hers possessively and this time there was no doubt or distrust to restrain her leaping senses as she responded to his hard, muscular body.

It was quite some time—Minnie was on her second pot of tea out in the saloon—before he said, 'You still haven't said you'll marry me. Would it persuade you if I suggested a honeymoon visit to Australia to see your family?'

'Luke! You don't mean it! Oh, that would be wonderful!' Her eyes were brilliant and she didn't think it was necessary to tell him she would marry him anyway, without any such inducement.

## COOKING WITH HERBS

As a gourmet cook, Jessamy no doubt knows that the key to turning a plain dish into memorable cuisine is the effective use of herbs. Not only do herbs add flavor and provide that extra hint of aroma or coloring, they are also rich in vitamins and aid digestion.

Following is a list of the more popular herbs and the foods they best enhance. Remember that the object is not to overwhelm natural flavors, so a pinch is often all you need.

| HERBS | FOODS |
| --- | --- |
| anise | sweet rolls, breads, fruit pies, shellfish |
| basil | sauces, salads, tomatoes, seafood, eggs |
| bay | stews, stuffings, sauces, meat, seafood, poultry |
| caraway | borscht, cabbage soup, breads, cookies, dips, cheese spreads |
| coriander | pea and chicken soups, pastries, dressings, Spanish dishes |
| dill | dips, dressings, potato salad, chowders, cottage cheese |
| garlic | meats, sauces, stews, Italian, Spanish and Greek dishes |
| mustard | salads, dressings, sauces, fish, soups, spreads, eggs |
| oregano | green salads, omelets, Italian and Mexican dishes |
| rosemary | stuffings, marinades, sauces, green salads, poultry |
| sage | pork, lamb stuffings, fish chowders, consommés |
| tarragon | seafood, chowders, chicken soup, sauces, salads, marinades, veal, poultry, eggs |
| thyme | brown sauces, pickled beets, fricassees, meat, poultry, creole and gumbo dishes |